AGENT RED (FATAL TARGET)

Teagan Stone Book 2

AVA S. KING

Latest Releases: Ava S. King

Agent Red Book 1 Teagan Stone
Agent Red Book 2 Teagan Stone

Upcoming Releases (2021/2022)
Agent Red Book 3 Teagan Stone
Agent Red Book 4 Teagan Stone
Mirror of Lies-Coming in 2022

I want to dedicate this book to my family and friends.

You're always with me, no matter where I go, and everything you've taught me has made me a better person.

Disclaimer

<hr>

This work of fiction contains strong language and explicit content and is only intended for mature readers. The story may contain unconventional situations, language, and sexual encounters that may offend some readers. This book is for mature readers (18+).

Introduction

Sign-up to Ava S. King's mailing list for news, new releases, and special offers.

https://landing.mailerlite.com/webforms/landing/r7j2s6

Synopsis

Teagan is used to uncovering secrets, but then she uncovers a plot that threatens to not only bring her harm but her family and her team. Making matters worse, the threat is painfully close to her.

She's in a race against time to prevent the next prime minister of Spain's swearing-in and the biggest threat in the history of the country. As the seasoned spy struggles to regain more of her memory and put the pieces of the high-stakes election day together, she's put to the ultimate test—one that she might not survive.

Can she unravel the convoluted mess before innocents are slaughtered in a land far away?

Chapter One

Spain 1 year later

Sweat beads dripped down Teagan's face as she raced down the US Embassy's dark hallway in Spain; it was going on almost midnight. The rest of her team was back at the checkpoint, while Spider sat in the caravan parked outside. She noticed as a flashlight came across the office window when she canvassed the US ambassador's office in Spain. Tegan hurried, turning her key light off, closing the file cabinet as quietly as possible, and left the room. As she darted down the hall, a voice called out, and she took off running to hide.

"Station one, do you see anything on the cameras?" The security guard radioed for assistance. He was around five-eight, shaved head, with tattoos he kept covered up. A former officer, he now worked as security after leaving the force to spend more time with his family.

"Negative, what's going on?" Dean, the onsite supervisor, questioned.

"Could be nothing, but I thought I heard something in one of the offices."

"Probably the cleaning crew, Thomas," Dean told him.

"Maybe, let me check the rest of the floor," Thomas said and continued walking over to each door and checked the handle to make sure they locked it. Teagan was slumped down under the door handle, praying he'd walk by without coming inside like he did the other doors. The office window was slightly ajar, and a breeze blew the vertical blinds back and forth, causing an echo throughout the floor. Thomas stepped in front of the last door and lifted his hand to slide the key inside.

"Are you on your way back?" Dean said, interrupting him.

"I was checking the last room; Cassandra left the window open," Thomas replied.

"Leave it alone and head back. I need you to cover the second floor," Dean told.

"All right," Thomas responded, removed the key, and stuck it back in his pocket. Teagan relaxed for the very first time. She stood to open the door slightly and look out to see Thomas gone. She slid her hoodie over her, keeping her face hidden, and turned to avoid the cameras. The first two weeks of surveillance showed them the hot spots to avoid. Finally, taking the stairs out of the building, she contemplated her next move. Possibly getting a staff position would help make things easier, but Teagan needed to be with her family. She was no longer taking missions that would put long periods of distance between them. Right then, she pushed the gate open to leave the embassy.

"Hey!" Thomas shouted. Teagan looked back.

"Fuck!" Teagan mumbled to herself and took off running as Thomas radioed about a breach in the building. Teagan ran as fast as she could toward the front gate, passing by the security guard who was sleeping from the drug she had injected him with so she could get inside the building.

Pop! Pop!

Gunfire startled Spider and caused him to go for his gun. He checked the chamber before starting the van and pulling up to the tree-covered rear side of the building with less camera access.

Teagan was almost out of harm's way when a bullet grazed her in the shoulder.

"Arghh!" she screamed, continuing to safety when Spider turned the car's headlights off.

"Go! Go!" Teagan shouted at Spider to drive as she eased down further in the seat to keep herself from being seen. More gunshots went off, hitting the taillight of the van. Spider rushed through the traffic light, made a sharp right turn, drove near the Ruben Dario subway station, and stopped. He parked the car and turned toward her to check her wound.

"We need to have you checked out," Spider demanded, and Teagan waved him off.

"I'm fine; it's just a scrape. Dump the van, and we'll head back to the hut," Teagan said.

Spider looked around the area; they were about ten minutes away from being back with the team.

"Try to keep the pressure on it while I get us to the next checkpoint," Spider stated, tore off the left sleeve of his t-shirt, and pulled off the road, driving another fifteen minutes to a tow truck yard. They'd scoped it out during their early research for when anything went wrong, and they needed to split up. He got out, stalked around to help lift Teagan, then shut the door. Spider walked up to an old Volkswagen that had a sign on top. He grabbed a rock off the ground, busted the window out, and unlocked the door. He climbed inside and hot-wired the engine as Teagan slid in on the passenger side with more sweat running down her face.

"Almost got it," Spider said, and the car turned on, and he hit the lights. Spider put on his seatbelt as they drive off in the opposite direction of the consulate. Spider pulled out his cell phone and texted a code.

Spider: Four.

Unknown: Received.

Spider tucked his phone back in his pocket and glanced back at Teagan. He snapped his fingers in her face to keep her awake.

"I'm good, Spider," Tegan explained, feeling groggier and shaking from the chills.

"It was just the one bullet, right?" Spider questioned, and Teagan nodded in answer. She was thinking over her years in the Navy, fighting for her country, dodging bullets and bombs. Still dealing with memory loss, Teagan wasn't a hundred percent back. Christian and she talked about taking a vacation soon with the kids. CJ, Cole, and Tatum were growing up fast. Holding those memories while they were still young was the most important thing to them as a couple. They knew how moving from one city or country to another put a strain on their development and meeting friends. It was the main reason Teagan wanted to leave first and become a full-time wife and mother. She had a few good years of having an everyday life without interruption until that fateful day she was taken away from her family and woke up chained to a bed. Her family was back in the States under protection while she worked on an assignment. She hadn't spoken to Christian in two days, and she promised to read Tatum a good night story every night.

The car turned down the street toward Calle Benidorm, twenty-nine apartments of the dark alleyway, of what they've called home for the past two weeks. Spider slid out of the driver's side as Gregory came out the side exit to help Teagan up the stairs. When Spider texted earlier, it was to make sure Doctor Raina was here to help. She didn't go on many missions out of the country, but Teagan requested to have someone with the skills necessary to handle any issue, so they wouldn't need a hospital unless it were an extreme emergency. Gregory lifted her left arm and put it around his shoulder as they strolled up the stairs. The narrow hallway with the burnt-out light led them to the apartment. He eased the door open as Raina placed her tools to clean Teagan's wound.

"Grab some more towels," Doctor Raina requested as she helped Teagan to lie on top of the covered table.

"She said it's just a graze," Spider spoke, dropping the towels next to the couch.

Raina removed the flashlight from her bag. The room had the basic couch, table, and chairs. A small kitchen with a fridge and stove, window curtain, sofa, and a four-seat table and lamp. Each took turns monitoring the area so the other one could sleep. Gregory brought over a blanket to cover Teagan from the waist down.

"What do you think?" Spider questioned Raina.

"She'll be fine; she mostly needs rest and water," Raina stated.

"Will she be ready to move in a day or two?" Gregory wondered, glancing at Teagan shivering on the table.

"I told her she shouldn't jump back in so fast. Her memory loss is something she needs to deal with," Raina said.

"We both know Teagan is stubborn," Spider said. The door opened with Broderick and Daughtrey entering.

"Can you get her to talk?" Broderick asked.

"She needs rest. Teagan probably hasn't eaten or slept properly since taking on the director position," Raina fussed, cleaning her wound.

"Which was her choice if you forgot," Broderick argued back.

"Can you not be an ass for a second, Broderick," Spider spat.

Daughtrey tapped him on the shoulder and whispered in his ear. The mission wouldn't be asa easy a task as he wanted. Broderick wasn't looking to take orders from Teagan any longer. He fought nonstop to get the director of The Firm's position, but the president wouldn't change his mind. Too much had transpired, and the only reason he was still around was that he had excellent skills as a fighter and shooter.

"She asked for this position. If she's not one hundred percent by tomorrow, I'm calling it into The Firm," Broderick stated and tried to walk off when Teagan grabbed his arm. They both stared into each other's eyes in a challenge. He jerked out of her hold and walked out of the room, leaving Daughtrey, Gregory, and Spider talking with Raina about the next steps for the mission.

"Do you think she was compromised?" Daughtrey questioned.

"I'm not sure. Suddenly, gunshots rang out, and she ran out of the building," Spider explained.

"Hopefully, she can tell us tomorrow," Gregory stated.

"If not, we will need to head back home and figure out another way," Daughtrey reminded.

Chapter Two

The next day, Teagan was up, showered, and refreshed. Raina forced her to eat a huge breakfast after she slept until noon. Wanting to hear from her family, she pulled the cell phone out of her bag and dialed the number.

"Hello," Christian spoke.

"Good to hear your voice," Teagan stated.

"What's wrong?" he asked.

Teagan stood in front of the window behind the curtain, watching the kids playing in the park across the street.

"I haven't talked to you or the kids in two days."

"CJ kept me up all night asking me when you're coming home," Christian sighed. Teagan closed her eyes, momentarily soaking in the silence.

"It won't be much longer," she announced.

"I thought this was finished years ago, Teagan. Why do you need to be there?" Christian questioned.

She asked herself that question all the time and tried to come up with the best way to answer her husband. Leaving The Firm wasn't as simple as he thought. Teagan knew she was chosen because she was the best at what she did. Bringing down corrupt leaders and stopping terrorist groups that tried to bring harm to American soil was a battle that would never stop.

"Where are the kids now?" Teagan asked, strolling to the edge of her bed and sitting to put her shoes on.

"CJ is playing a video game with Cole, and Tatum's with my mom," Christian answered. Christian's mom was always visiting, even when she didn't call and popped up, expecting them to drop everything to accommodate her.

"Tell them I'll be home soon and kiss them for me," Teagan suggested, her phone tucked between her shoulder and ear.

"I miss you," Christian replied.

"I miss you too," Teagan suggested as a knock came at the door.

"Call me when you're on your way home," Christian responded.

"Come in!" Teagan called out.

Spider walked inside her room.

"Babe, let me call you back," Teagan remarked and ended the call.

"How are you feeling?" Spider asked, checked her bandaged arm. She wore black jeans, a white shirt, and tactical boots.

"Good, ready to get this over with. Is everybody here?" She stood and grabbed the bulletproof vest, shirt, and black hoodie.

"Yeah. Listen, if you need more time, we can reschedule," Spider stated.

"I'll be fine," Teagan said.

"Well, after last night, we need to keep an eye on you," Spider explained and headed to the front of the apartment. Teagan followed, and Raina packed up her things.

"Thanks again, Raina," Teagan said.

"Don't thank me. Be careful," Raina mentioned, lifting her medical bag. Daughtrey and Gregory sat at the kitchen table, reading over paperwork and drinking coffee.

"Where's Broderick?" Teagan said, opening the fridge to grab a bottle of water.

"Bringing the van around," Daughtrey said, passing Teagan the newspaper.

The headline read, *Suspicious Person at US Embassy - Security Spiked.*

"Any word on if they have any pictures of me?" Teagan said.

Gregory and Daughtrey shared a look.

"They think it was a woman, but nothing close up," Gregory said.

"Great."

The swearing-in was in two months. Teagan needed to find out all she could about the incoming prime minister. If the US ambassador worked together with Spain to plot against America, it would cause a ripple effect across many countries. The president sent her in after an anonymous recording came across The Firm's desk with the incoming prime minister talking about taking over the Senate with his elected candidates. The money trail was still overwhelming, with a lot to go through. Teagan respected the office of the presidency no matter who was elected. Her first allegiance was to protect the interests of the United States, and now to have a coup about to happen was something she didn't see coming after being pulled back into the fire of The Firm. After burying Leah and heading back home to her family, Teagan read up on what had been happening at The Firm, specifically what changes Stanton had put in place. As the new director, she had to dismantle the corruption and rebuild an organization to what it should be by taking down any known enemies of America.

"We need to take it a step further and make contact," Teagan said.

"Wait; what?" Daughtrey said.

Teagan pointed at the map of the embassy.

"Hear me out."

"What you're saying is to compromise this mission," Broderick spoke, closing the door.

"What I'm saying is make contact. Rattle the ambassador."

Spider stood back, nodding in agreement.

"You agree with this bullshit," Broderick said.

"I think it could work," Spider said, grabbing the photos of the US ambassador off the table. Broderick shook his head, not believing it after last night when she was grazed by a bullet. She wanted to go back in like nothing happened. He was still walking on eggshells in The Firm after his role in Diablo's situation. Once Teagan became entrenched in reworking the organization's structure, she made sure Broderick was still under her watchful eye.

"What if the security guard who shot you is still there?" Broderick announced.

"We go in with our badges," Teagan said, sliding her cell out of her pocket to check the time. Moving back to New York and working from the general office was the only thing on her mind after this mission. Now that some of her memory was coming back slowly, with the help of therapy, she promised her husband and family that she wouldn't continue putting her life on the line. At thirty-one, Teagan was hopeful that she could hand over everything to Spider if he wanted the responsibility in a year or two. Daughtrey stood, packing up the rest of the documents, and Gregory loaded more weapons.

"What if he doesn't take the bait?" Broderick said.

"If he's anything like you, Broderick, I suspect he will," Teagan said and strolled toward the back of the apartment toward her room to grab her gun. The friendship she had early on with Broderick was no longer there; trust was broken, and she looked at everyone now with the mindset that at any moment, they would sell her out. Even Spider, someone she grew to call a brother. Now, the only people she would put her life on the line for were her husband and kids. When Teagan slid her gun in her holster and picked up her badge and ID, she turned to walk out of the room, but Broderick blocked the door.

"I'm not the enemy, Teagan," he said.

"I wish I could believe that, Broderick," she responded.

"You know more than anyone. This organization takes until you have nothing left," he argued.

"What I know is that you were plotting behind the team's back."

He chuckled and shook his head.

"Diablo was right about you."

Teagan's eyebrows narrowed into slits.

"What did you say?"

"Nothing," Broderick replied and stalked away with Teagan following.

Everyone was suited up, marching out of the apartment during daylight from the back alleyway. Spider stayed alert and watched as everyone loaded into the van, and Gregory got in the driver's side. Spider made sure the temporary plumbing label was a legit business they could use when deciding to take over the full surveillance time from the other men who were sent from the agency earlier. Gregory turned the van at the end of the corner and pulled off to head into traffic down the street past the subway station they came across earlier that night.

"Daughtrey, I should go inside since they don't know our faces," Broderick remarked.

"No, you two stay outside. Spider and I will go in together," Teagan replied, looking out the window at the cars going by.

"If they have you on camera?" Broderick questioned.

"We use it to our advantage," Teagan stated, rubbing her arm, still feeling the pain from the graze.

"Broderick might be right, Teagan," Spider said, looking over the map of the embassy.

"I don't doubt he might be right, but we need to push this case further. We're two months away, and things aren't escalating fast," Teagan responded.

Thirty minutes later, Gregory pulled up on the side of the embassy and kept the van running. Teagan, Spider, and Broderick stepped out.

"Where are you going?" Teagan asked, holding her hand up, blocking him.

"Inside with you. I know I'm not your biggest fan right now, but you need me in there," Broderick said. Teagan looked over her shoulder at Spider, and he nodded in acknowledgment. Teagan sighed, agreeing to let him follow along.

"Keep the van running; if you see anything, text," Teagan remarked.

"Will do, Boss," Daughtrey joked, saluting as Teagan said nothing; she just stared at him blankly while chewing the inside of her mouth. She was used to men never taking her seriously in the field, but over the years, she earned the respect of the generals and leaders around the world for the work she did when she was knee deep in fighting America's rights abroad. All three of them walked up to the security station and held their badges up.

"How can I help you?" the security personnel standing in the booth asked.

"We need to speak with the ambassador," Teagan said.

"Do you have an appointment?" he asked.

"Yes," Teagan replied, shocking Broderick and Spider.

Teagan was ten steps ahead of everyone and made an appointment a week ago after the property's first surveillance. She knew at some point they would need to speak with the ambassador to test the waters.

"What's your name?" the security guard asked.

"Detective Teagan Stone."

The security guard typed her name into the computer, and it popped up: she was a detective in the US working on a case about human trafficking. Gregory was on the team who was skilled in creating fake documents, so everything looked legit when traced back to a fake IP address.

"All right, take this visitor badge," Jimmy said as he printed out three visitor badges for them, and they walked up to the elevator and headed up to the office of Ambassador Cedric Fenton. The doors opened. Teagan led the team down the hall with the ambassador's assistant, meeting them at the elevator after Jimmy called.

"Hello, Detective Stone. I'm Amber Mason, assistant to Ambassador Fenton," Amber said and smiled. Teagan extended her hand for a shake as she scanned the room, looking at the active conversations as all eyes were on them.

"Hi, is the ambassador available?" Teagan asked.

"He has a few minutes he can speak with you before his next meeting," Amber said. She turned toward the door, knocked lightly, and peeked inside. Cedric was on the phone, but he waved them inside as he leaned back in his seat and laughed at something said. Teagan, Broderick, and Spider stood and waited for another five minutes. He finally ended his call and peered over at the three people standing in front of him wearing combat gear.

"Ambassador Fenton, I'm Detective Stone," Teagan spoke, motioning to take a seat, and he replied with a nod.

"What can I do for you, Detective?" Cedric responded, leaning over the desk and clasping his hands together. Cedric, in his late forties, was a former investment banker in California who made his money lobbying for drug companies and eventually making his way into Congress with close ties to Senate Majority Leader Larry Coleman, the person blocking every bill the president brought to both houses of government.

"My team and I are investigating human trafficking cases that we traced back to Spain, particularly near the embassy," Teagan spoke, watching as Cedric's eyes wandered over the room, with his sunken eyebrows, biting his bottom lip. She tried to turn off reading people's body language; it was an old habit she used when interrogating suspects.

Cedric cleared his throat.

"How can my office help, Detective Stone?" he asked.

"We'd like to get case files on all of your employees," Teagan said, knowing he would deny that request.

"I can't do that," Cedric replied.

"Have you noticed anyone coming in late consistently, or gone for long periods of time?" Teagan asked.

"No."

"What about yourself?" she replied.

He glared at her, questioning, "What?!"

"Hope I didn't offend you, Ambassador. We have to ask everyone these questions."

"What agency are you with again?"

"I didn't say," Teagan replied.

Chapter Three

Cedric picked up his phone to make a call, and Teagan stopped him before he could dial for security.

"We're here under strict orders. It would be best to hold our identities from your team," Teagan said.

"I'm not comfortable with you investigating my staff," Cedric explained, hanging up the phone. One thing The Firm taught the team was to implant doubt in each suspect. Either of themselves or the people around them. Get them isolated and away from any type of comfortable position to get a free out.

"I understand, but Mr. Fenton, as you know, the only way to weed out corruption is to find the root cause," Teagan answered, peering into his eyes.

"Why do I feel like I'm being investigated," Cedric commented.

"Sir, we have no doubt that you have America's interests in high regard," Broderick stated.

Teagan allowed Broderick to distract Cedric with conversation. From reading Cedric's file, she learned that he was on his third marriage with four kids. Taking a women's opinion would be the last thing she expected him to do. Working her way up in the agency was always met with hesitation from her male counterparts. In their eyes, she only made it because she was sleeping her way to the top, not because she was smart, skilled, and strong in being a marksman and a fighter.

"I've been at this job for a long time," Cedric remarked, shifting in his seat.

"Over fifteen years," Teagan stated.

"We had a breach the other night; someone was lurking in the office building," Cedric recalled.

"Our team can look into that if you'd like."

"Detective Stone, there's a high probability this has nothing to do with the embassy," Cedric said, typing on his computer and printing out statements from the breach last night.

"I think you're right, but it's best to take everything into consideration," she said, taking the paperwork out of his hands.

"I'm aware this will take time, but we can't have you questioning my staff," Cedric said.

"Have you spoken with the prime minister about this?" Cedric inquired, sparking up an opening that Teagan was hoping would lead down the road of him telling on himself.

"The prime minister swearing in is coming up soon," Broderick mentioned.

"Will you be discreet, Mr. Fenton?" Teagan asked.

Spider tapped Broderick on the shoulder.

"Mr. Fenton, have you spoken with the incoming prime minister?" Teagan remarked, standing.

"Briefly when he won the election," Cedric said. A knock came to the door, and Amber entered.

"Mr. Fenton, your next appointment is here," Amber said.

"Thank you, Amber," Cedric replied, grabbing his file folders. Teagan glanced around the room.

"Mr. Fenton, do you mind if I use your phone?" Teagan asked. Cedric stood at the door, turned, and looked over his shoulder.

"You can use my assistant's phone," Cedric told her.

"It'll only be a second, sir. I promise not to steal anything," Teagan teased, chuckling when Spider and Broderick smiled.

Cedric looked at Broderick and Spider, then back at Teagan. They worked for the same government in his mind. Nothing suspicious about that.

"Sure. Amber will stay behind if you need anything," Cedric explained.

Teagan looked at Broderick and nodded, heading to Amber. He kept his hand on the doorknob and his right hand on the wall, blocking Amber from watching Teagan insert a USB drive into Cedric's computer. Teagan pretended to make a call, while Spider wandered over to the filing cabinet.

"How long have you worked here, Amber?" Broderick asked.

"Uh… maybe five years," Amber said.

"You're cute," Broderick said, pushing a piece of her hair behind her ear. She smiled.

"Thank you," Amber responded, twisting her ponytail.

"Is that your desk?" Broderick pointed at the brown desk with photos of a child and an older woman laughing together on a swing.

Broderick led Amber over to her desk and closed the door. Spider opened the top cabinet and looked through the files, trying to find anything incriminating. Teagan opened each drawer, except the bottom one wouldn't budge. Teagan tried to look around for a key or something to get it open.

Teagan's flash drive finished downloading, and she pulled it from the computer when Amber returned.

"All done," Teagan stated, standing.

Spider held a folder behind his back.

"Do you need help to find your way rout?" Amber questioned.

"Nope. We'll figure it out," Teagan said.

"Mr. Fenton said if you have any more questions, to take his business card," Amber said.

Teagan took the card from her hand.

"Amber, how long have you worked for Mr. Fenton?"

"Five years, give or take," Amber answered.

"How is your relationship?" Teagan said, hitting the button of the elevator.

"He's been a great boss. Is there something I should know?" Amber replied, arms folded over her chest.

"Nothing in particular. We've had a few cases of women coming up missing," Teagan blurted out in front of everyone. The entire room went silent.

"You don't think Mr. Fenton had anything to do with that, right?" Amber responded.

"We go where the evidence takes us," Teagan said, leaving Amber speechless, and headed to the elevator as the doors closed.

"What do you think?" Spider said. Teagan sighed, leaning against the back wall of the elevator.

"I think he knows that we're on to him," Teagan answered. When the door opened, they stepped out and strolled out of the building. Not paying attention to where she was walking, she bumped into the security guard who shot at her last night.

"Oh, sorry. Teagan said.

"No problem," he said and did a double take as the door closed.

Teagan looked forward, heading to the van.

"Hey, do I know you?" a voice called out, and all three of them looked back.

Teagan lifted her hand to block out the sun.

"Sorry, I don't recall," Teagan responded, opening the passenger side door of the van.

They all watched as he stared back at the van as Gregory pulled out into traffic and drove away.

"He might be a problem," Broderick stated.

"We haven't moved on yet."

"I agree with Broderick this time," Spider commented.

Teagan leaned against the window, reading over the file Spider took out of the cabinet. It was a file copy of Matias transferring money into an account to a nonprofit organization called *Children Smile.*

"Where to now?" Gregory asked.

"I need to speak with the president," Teagan spoke.

All the documents showed it was established two years ago when Matias was looking to get into politics, and Cedric was in debt for over ten million dollars.

The van made it back to the apartment, and they piled out and headed back upstairs. Teagan passed the drive to Gregory who added it to the secured computer. She slid the phone out of her pocket and dialed the secret code to the president's secure line.

"Hello."

"May I speak with the president?" Teagan said, standing next to Gregory.

"One moment please," the secretary said.

"Teagan," President Sanders said.

"Mr. President, we just met with Cedric Fenton."

"Did he say anything?" Sanders spoke.

Gregory pointed at the screen showing a map of the swearing-in location and the people attending. Tegan bent down, muffled the phone, and asked to zoom in on the map.

"We know Cedric is working with Matias."

"Send me the evidence," President Sanders stated.

"Coming through right now to you, sir."

"I can't stress this enough; we only have two months before the swearing-in ceremony."

"Yes, sir. Are you meeting with him?"

"It's on my schedule to call and congratulate him. Even though I think he bought this election," Sanders remarked.

"If he's selling us out, we need to monitor him and Cedric," Broderick brought up, sitting on the couch and checking his messages.

"I need you all back here soon," President Sanders stated.

"We need more support out here if we go in without his," Teagan said, grabbing water out of the fridge.

"Call the Joint Chiefs and get us all on the line together," President Sanders responded.

"I can fly to DC while the guys oversee the events."

"Get here soon. The minute he finds out you're on to him..." Sanders said.

"I know, Mr. President," Teagan spoke then hung up the phone, rubbing her forehead.

"Do you remember a black car sitting across the street?" Spider said, standing at the window and looking out.

"What are they doing?" Teagan asked, strolling next to him. Kids were playing in the yard. An older woman carrying groceries walked down the street with her younger daughter next to her eating ice cream. Teagan watched for a few more minutes before she decided to make a move.

"Take Gregory with you and be discreet." Teagan made another call to get a flight to DC. Gregory and Spider grabbed guns and vests as they walked out of the apartment.

"Hey," Christian answered.

Teagan logged into the laptop on the kitchen table that Gregory was using. She went to the United Airlines website to make arrangements to fly to DC.

"I'm flying to DC for a few days." Teagan told.

"How much longer is this case?" Christian asked.

"The swearing in is in two months, and then we're back home."

"The kids miss you; I miss you," Christian stated.

"I know."

Pop! Pop!

Loud gunfire went off, startling the team. Teagan dropped her phone and ran to the window.

"Shit!" Teagan yelled, rushing to pick up her phone.

"What's going on, Teagan?" Christian questioned.

Broderick marched to the door, and Teagan pulled him back to wait a minute.

"Christian, let me call you back," Teagan said and hung up.

Chapter Four

Daughtrey came up behind her with two extra nine-millimeter guns, and he passed one to Teagan. She motioned for Broderick to take the lead and Daughtrey the back. They'd been compromised, so the next route was to get her men to leave town together and send new people out to keep a watch on the embassy and the prime minister's residence. He paused, nudging the door gently, and looked at Gregory. Spider stood next to an old, broken-down car returning fire at the black car on the opposite street with the mother and daughter caught in the middle. Broderick eased his way out the door and went to the right. He sent shots to the two men across the street to give Spider a little relief. Teagan followed and went over to the back of the car, dodging bullets and trying to see how she could bring the mother and daughter to safety.

"What happened?" Teagan shouted, popping her head up to see over the hood of the car. The woman prayed and cried as she covered her daughter. Teagan came back down, thinking of her next move.

"We came outside to walk toward the van."

"They just started shooting?" Teagan questioned.

"Yeah," Spider said.

Pop! Pop!

Teagan tapped Spider on the shoulder as she looked to her left then right. She jumped up, trying to distract the men from shooting.

"Over here!" Teagan shouted.

They noticed Teagan and shot toward her as a car drove down the road and almost hit the mother and daughter.

"Shit!" Teagan spat. She pulled her gun out, shooting at the tires of the car to get them to go in the other direction. The car crashed in the back of another parked on the small street. Teagan pulled the family up and took them to the alleyway for safety.

"Thank you! Thank you," the mother said, hugging her daughter.

"You're welcome," Teagan replied and went back to her team as they walked up on the two men dead in the middle of the road.

"Check their IDs," Broderick spoke.

"We don't have much time. The police will be here soon," Teagan said, raising her hand over her brow to block out the sun. Broderick tossed her the wallet he had found in the man's back pocket.

"This isn't a random hit," Broderick said, running a hand through his hair.

Teagan scanned the ID that showed they were local police. What were the odds that two policemen would be outside their apartment building causing a shootout in broad daylight? She noticed he had a piece of paper in his wallet with the address of their apartment and door number.

"Who do you think sent him?" Spider asked, picking the ID out of her hands.

"Has to be the ambassador," Teagan remarked and gave Spider the rest of the wallet.

"All right, time to get out of here," Broderick said as sirens went off, indicating police were coming. Teagan, Gregory, and the rest of them ran back in the building and up the stairs to pack up their bags.

"What about the mother and daughter?" Broderick questioned.

"What about them?" Teagan responded, lifting her bag from the floor and piling the rest of her things inside.

"They can point us out," Broderick said, packing his gun and looking over the room to see if he had dropped anything else. Gregory closed all the computers they had running in the room and packed them up while Daughtrey handled tossing the food out of the fridge.

"We're not killing a mother and daughter, Broderick." Spider grabbed her bag, ran downstairs to the back alley, and threw her stuff inside with the other luggage.

"Get rid of your burner phones," Teagan said, opening a trash bag. They all tossed them inside after taking out the sim card and stomping a foot on top of them. Everyone walked out of the apartment and shut the door, strolling down the back stairs to the van.

"It doesn't have to be us," Broderick replied and climbed into the backseat of the van. Teagan tied the trash bag with the cell phones. Spider closed the door and hopped in on the passenger side as Daughtrey started the van. He jumped into traffic, mixing in with other cars to throw off anyone from following the team.

"That's not happening, Broderick. We have enough on our plate." Teagan typed on her phone to see if she could get the president on the phone.

Teagan: Code Red

Unknown: Call me.

"Gregory got us some flights out of here now. Spider, contact the ambassador," Teagan ordered and waited for a response to her text.

"Sir, we've been compromised," Teagan said.

"How did this happen?" the president asked, whispering to someone in the background.

"I think it's the ambassador."

"He wouldn't move that fast," the president stated.

"I'm afraid we can't be so sure. I think we tipped him off." Daughtrey changed lanes and hopped on the freeway.

"Get back here now, and we'll refocus. Congress will be in session soon," the president replied.

Teagan glanced again over her shoulder and noticed a police car behind them. It could be nothing or a threat that they'd been caught.

"Yes, sir," Teagan said and ended the call. Daughtrey caught Teagan's worried expression in the rearview mirror.

"I see the car, Teagan. Should I take it out?" Daughtrey asked.

"Not yet. Take the fastest route to the airport."

Daughtrey nodded in answer, changing lanes to get off the main freeway. They were a few miles away from Madrid International airport. Daughtrey sped up when the same police car followed and turned their sirens on.

"He's on our tail," Daughtrey mentioned.

"We can't get caught here," Teagan spoke, glancing over her shoulder.

Understanding, Daughtrey continued driving, moving in and out of traffic. Passing cars to put a little distance between them.

"I'm going to get you guys close, and you jump out," Daughtrey said.

"Do we have the tickets?" Spider asked.

Teagan was still checking her email for verification of the plane tickets. She shook her head at Spider.

"What's the plan?" Spider asked.

"What did the ambassador say?"

"He's out at a meeting," Spider replied, pissed at having no idea where things would land for the team if they got stuck in Spain in police custody.

"He's honking at us," Daughtrey said.

"Can you lose him?" Teagan called out, noticing a second police car approaching them. Daughtrey sped over to the cab area to mix in with the crowd. Everyone stayed alert.

Teagan leaned over and passed over a bag. Her cell phone vibrated.

Unknown: You have your tickets and security clearance.

Teagan: Thank you, sir.

"Tickets are set. Follow me."

"What about clearance for our guns?" Spider remarked, opening the passenger door.

"All good. Daughtrey, hurry up and lose them. Cause a small incident if you can and get to American Airlines in ten minutes," Teagan said, patting him on the shoulder and taking his bag.

"Teagan, if I don't …" Daughtrey replied.

"Don't even think like that," Teagan told.

Teagan slammed the door shut and followed Spider and the rest of the team as they went through security, holding up their IDs. As they passed through, she noticed the second police car stop, get out of the car, and come toward the entrance. She nudged Spider to look over her shoulder as a loud crash was heard.

"OMG!" a woman with her husband yelled, pointing at the van Daughtrey was driving as it crashed into a cab. The driver was yelling at an empty van.

"He'll make it," Spider said as they walked further down the airport toward American Airlines.

Teagan picked up her pace as much as possible without drawing attention as they moved through the crowd. Finally getting in line, Teagan pulled up the tickets and noticed it stated first class.

"Hello, we're now boarding first class," the ticket counter called out. Daughtrey came running up out of breath. Spider shook hands with him as Teagan held up her ID and ticket. The door opened for everyone to walk onto the plane.

"Did you lose the police?" Broderick whispered in Daughtrey's ear.

"Yeah, but we need to get out of here fast," Daughtrey said, holding up his ID.

Chapter Five

The attendant called for everyone to take a seat. Teagan pushed her bag under her seat and sat next to Gregory and Spider while Broderick and Daughtrey sat across from them. The doors of the plane shut as everyone got comfortable, and the stewardess called for everyone to turn off devices and buckle their seats.

"Drinks and snacks will be offered soon," the flight attendant announced.

Daughtrey placed his headphones in his ears and showed Broderick the music he was listening to on his phone. He shrugged and glanced out the window.

"We need to meet with the president," Spider stated. The light popped on for everyone to prepare for takeoff. Out of the corner of Teagan's eyes, she saw a few policemen crowd the desk, talking with the flight crew and motioning at the plane as they left the runway. Teagan laid her head back on the seat, thinking of the next steps of the operation as the new director. Taking on so much responsibility was a big issue she hadn't thought about when she told the president about how things needed to change. The corruption and destruction they'd done over the years weighed heavy on her heart as she progressed at the agency. Her parents always told her that she didn't know how to just let things go and would take on everybody's problems. Now here she was, going back into the life she had run away from: the constant travel around the country, killing, and destruction to keep her country safe. To keep her family safe. Teagan's breath snagged hold on something inside her chest. She closed her eyes, trying to catch up on some sleep. Since the beginning of her mission, she'd been going nonstop, from being deep undercover, surveillance, and planning to bring down Hernandez.

The alarm went off on her nightstand, and Teagan still wouldn't move. She felt a small tap on her shoulder and slowly opened her eyes. Teagan smiled back at the wide grin of her son as he stood in front of her, wearing his Paw Patrol pajamas. The flight came in late the day before, and she'd been sleeping ever since. She had asked her husband to keep the kids busy and away from the bedroom to give her some time to relax and re-assimilate from being gone. Teagan pushed the blanket back and tapped on the bed for him to climb up and cuddle.

"Mommy, when did you get home?" Cole asked, lifted his head, and stared at his mom.

Teagan pulled him to her chest, kissed the top of his head, and rubbed his back.

"I came home late, baby."

"Did you bring me anything back?" Cole looked up into her eyes and grinned with his missing tooth that recently fell out while she was away. Normally, she would handle everything with the kids while he worked, but now that she was back in the fold of The Firm, they decided that he would manage the kids' day-to-day duties, along with his parents helping when they could.

"Cole, why are you bothering your mother?" Her husband walked in the door holding a cup of coffee, dressed in a black business suit. He passed the cup to Teagan, and she sat up with her back to the headboard and grabbed it out of his hands.

"Mommy doesn't mind." Cole poked his bottom lip out in a pout. Teagan shook her head and bent down to kiss his cheek.

"Go eat your breakfast," Christian said, sliding his hands in his pockets.

Cole rose out of bed and stomped off to the kitchen. CJ and Tatum stayed under Christian, but Teagan and Cole were joined at the hip. Everything she did or everywhere she went, he wanted to follow. Teagan placed the cup of coffee down on the nightstand and clasped her hands together in her lap.

"Tired." He leaned his leg against the edge of the bed and reached out to tap the top of her hand.

"Exhausted."

"How did the mission go?"

"You know I can't talk about that." Teagan flashed a faint smile toward him.

He sighed, nodded, and pressed a kiss to her forehead, then her lips.

"I made breakfast. I know you're tired and have to get to the office, but it would be nice to have you sit with the kids."

"Let me shower, and I'll be out in a few minutes."

"How long this time?" he questioned.

Teagan jumped out of bed wearing Christian's large t-shirt.

"Huh."

"How long will you be gone this time?"

"Not long. Christian, you know this work changes constantly. I can't give a definite answer." Teagan strolled to the bathroom and turned on the shower. She stepped in front of the mirror and pinned her hair up. Christian stood at the entrance of the door and watched her in awe. After so many years, he still couldn't believe she was his wife and the mother of his children. Something about Teagan Stone brought out the protectiveness in him.

"I know, but this case is taking a lot longer than I expected."

Teagan turned and stood in front of him with her arms crossed over her chest.

"I promise once it's over, I'll take some time off."

"Maybe we can take a vacation."

"Wherever you want to go, I'll follow." Teagan stood on her tiptoes, pecked his lips, and went to step in the shower. Christian walked out of the bathroom and scratched the side of his cheek. He noticed her cell phone vibrating while on the charger. He picked it up, noticing the name flashed across.

"Hello." Christian looked back over his shoulder at the bathroom door.

"Christian, is Teagan there?" Spider asked.

"Uh, she's getting dressed."

"Can you tell her to call me as soon as she can?" Spider stated, blowing out a breath over the phone.

"Sure." The bathroom door opened, and Teagan stepped out with a towel wrapped around her body as she picked up the lotion off the dresser and sat on the bed.

"Spider just called."

"What did he say?" Teagan looked up at him.

"He didn't say."

"I'll call him back after breakfast." Teagan stood and wrapped her arms around Christian's waist.

"Thank you."

"You and the kids are my priority always." Teagan released him, treaded to the closet, and grabbed a pants suit to prepare for the meeting that would be called to discuss what happened in Spain.

Christian headed to the kitchen and saw the kids laughing and eating their breakfast while Paw Patrol played on the TV screen. Christian picked up his cup of coffee, took a sip, and grabbed a piece of bacon off his oldest son's plate.

"Daddy, is Mommy awake?" CJ asked, biting into his pancake. Teagan stepped inside and kissed all three of the kids on the top of their heads.

"Mmm, this smells good." Teagan grabbed a plate off the counter and filled it up with bacon, toast, pancakes, and eggs.

Teagan sat between Cole and Tatum and winked at Christian as he watched over his family at the head of the table.

"Morning, Mommy." Tatum lifted her glass of orange juice.

"Hey, baby. You been good for Daddy?" Teagan asked.

Tatum shrugged her shoulders. Christian chuckled, and Teagan giggled.

"Your daughter," Christian spoke.

"Takes after your mother." Teagan pointed her fork at Christian and rolled her eyes.

The conversations about CJ wanting to go on a school trip to the zoo with his friends at school continued. Teagan loved moments like this, having an average day in her life being a wife, mom, and daughter. Hanging with PTA moms and planning bake sales instead of going undercover as a spy.

"How long are you going to be gone today?" Christian inquired, helping Cole with cutting his pancakes.

"Hopefully not long. If I'm late, I'll call you about dinner." Teagan took the permission slip out of CJ's hand and signed her name. Christian nodded and listened to the back and forth arguing between Cole and Tatum.

Teagan left the house an hour later and pulled in front of a building that held no type of description. She removed her shades and walked up to the door as the camera scanned her face for entrance. It was a Friday morning at nine thirty as the door automatically opened. Teagan walked down the dark hallway as soldiers stood in formation carrying weapons. The Firm had many offices around the city, separate from the main office. Teagan planned on getting the guys back together for an early morning meeting before they broke off to spend time with their families. Spider stood over Gregory in the conference room with monitors displaying the entire city.

"Is he ready?" Teagan stepped in the room, and all eyes glanced at her. Daughtrey passed her a file folder and sat back down. Broderick came in behind her, talking on his phone, and sat next to Daughtrey.

"Uh, huh." Broderick grabbed a pen and notepad from the middle of the table.

"He's about to patch in any minute now." Spider pointed at the monitor for the president to come online. Broderick finished his call, put his phone away, and looked up at Teagan.

"I have a contact that said Hernandez and Fenton met again today."

"That's unfortunate." Teagan opened the folder and scanned over the photos of Matias' wife and child. If they needed to be pulled into the plan, she would make that as a last resort; handling children in these types of situations could get sticky.

"Agent Stone," the president remarked, sitting in front of the monitor in the situation room next to the chief of staff.

"Mr. President."

"What do you have for me?"

"The surveillance was compromised, but we did get out in time without anyone making a connection between you and us." Teagan pulled out the chair to take a seat.

"Do you believe you can pull this off?"

"Every mission is different, sir, but I trust my team."

"That's not enough confidence if you're trying to convince me."

"Sir, with all due respect, we're the best in the business."

"I don't want any blood on our hands."

"I never promise."

"Run the plan down for me."

Teagan motioned for Spider to talk.

"Mr. President, we have someone who can take over without being detected."

"Someone like who?"

"Acevedo Vasquez." Spider tapped Gregory to bring up his file on the screen.

"He's almost an exact duplicate of Hernandez." The president ran a hand down his face.

"Exactly. If we can get him to swap places, we can cut Fenton off before it gets out of hand," Spider explained, shuffling to the next photo of Fenton and Hernandez secretly meeting in an alleyway.

"How many men do you need?" the president questioned.

"The usual team and maybe a few on the inside," Teagan said.

"The US Embassy can't be compromised by this; the less our hands touch this the better for everyone."

"I understand, sir. We have phone calls between them to discuss plans to possibly plant people in the House of Representatives over a coup."

"He needs to be stopped," the president replied.

"That's our goal, sir."

Chapter Six

Spider ran over the directions for the infiltration of the palace for the president and the team. On the screen, black checkmarks signified which door they could use to slip in and out, knowing the best time to handle this would be during the swearing in when everyone was distracted.

"I'd like to hear the tapes now," the president said.

"Yes, sir." Gregory tapped on his keyboard, and a voice box popped up on the screen.

Fenton: I have everything worked out.

Hernandez: Mr. Ambassador, you know I can't be involved in this.

Fenton: You won't be if we pull this off the right way.

Hernandez: How do you think your president will feel about you turning on your country?

Fenton: My goal is to be the next president.

Hernandez chuckled over the phone.

Hernandez: If I become prime minister without any hiccups.

Fenton: Just send me the twenty million dollars.

Hernandez: It will be sent once the swearing in is over.

Fenton groaned over the phone, and Gregory cut the recording off.

"Have you looked into all of his accounts?" President Sanders wondered.

"Fenton tried hard to hide his money in offshore accounts, but Gregory was able to find some things."

"Why not all?" The president's face soured.

"He's using family members' names to hide some of his money. We don't want to tip them off," Teagan explained.

"All right, if he makes another move, let me know asap."

"Yes, Mr. President," Teagan stated, and Gregory ended the remote video call.

"If we mess this up, the president will cause an international incident," Broderick reminded them.

"You should know about those," Spider muttered, and he glared at him.

Teagan shook her head at her team members and stood.

"Paint the picture for me, Gregory. You're the tech expert, so how will this play out?" Teagan questioned.

Gregory leaned back in the chair in thought, rubbing his beard.

"If I can verify all the cameras, I can get us inside the palace and know what's going on at all times." Gregory looked over at her.

"Daughtrey, while Gregory is focused on the technology, where are you?" Teagan pointed at him.

"Transportation. I need at least two to three backup cars locked and loaded," Daughtrey rushed out.

"What about air?" Teagan tilted her head at him.

"Private jet with one of our guys flying," Daughtrey responded, taking notes.

Teagan tapped her chin and nodded, glancing at Broderick.

"Work on putting our people in place to replace Hernandez," Broderick said, and Teagan smirked.

"Good answer."

Spider crossed his arms and cleared his throat.

"I can handle finding out what's happening with Congress," Spider said, taking the folder off the table.

"Then I guess we're all on the same page. If you think you can't handle this, tell me now." Teagan looked around the room and peered at each one to get a sense of any hesitation.

"Any hesitation from you, Teagan?" Broderick asked.

"Always," Teagan replied and walked out of the conference room to allow everyone time to get to work.

Four hours later, Teagan was at the grocery store, grabbing food for the house. Christian texted that he wanted steak, lobster, mashed potatoes, and mac and cheese. He planned to invite his parents over. Teagan held out a notepad as she scratched off each item as she pushed the cart down the bread aisle. When Teagan's cell phone rang, she lifted it out of her pocket as she grabbed a bottle of sauce.

"Hello."

"Thank God you answered."

"Sasha?" Teagan questioned in shock to finally hear from one of her close friends who lived in the same neighborhood as her family. Sasha was married with two kids of her own; she was a regular mom who was still blind to what Teagan did in real life.

"Yes, where have you been? Christian said you've been out of town for a funeral," Sasha spoke, and Teagan chortled, knowing Christian hated lying, but he covered for her whenever she needed to leave on a mission.

"Sorry, I just got back yesterday. Been spending time with the kids."

"Well, I'm sorry for the loss of your Uncle Kevin."

"Who?" Teagan wondered.

"The funeral, your Uncle Kevin on your mom's side."

Teagan didn't have an uncle, but she had to play along with the lie to keep Sasha from asking more questions. Sasha was a great friend, but she could be a big gossiper if Teagan allowed that door to open. The entire neighborhood knew about each other's business from who was cheating, to who lost their job. Teagan wasn't that type of person to get in anybody's business, but over time, she became close with Sasha because of their kids, and their husbands were friends. It always surprised Teagan how Sasha and Stuart were happily married. He was the quiet type, and Sasha was outgoing, the life of the party. Somehow, they worked and had been married for over fifteen years.

"Oh yeah, Uncle Kevin. It was rough, but we made it through as a family."

"Where are you now?"

Teagan pushed the cart over to the next aisle. As her hand came down from the top shelf, she noticed a woman staring right at her.

"Huh."

Teagan put a box in her cart and glanced back up. The woman was no longer standing at the corner of the aisle. Teagan shook off the thought and finished collecting everything they needed for dinner.

"At the grocery store."

"Christian said his parents were coming for dinner."

"Yep. How about you and the family come over so we can catch up."

As she listened to Sasha run down her plans for tonight, she chuckled at her complaining about Stuart Jr. getting in trouble at school for talking during class.

"That child talks too much." Sasha blew out a breath.

"He takes after his mother." Teagan laughed, and Sasha chuckled over the phone.

Teagan placed her things on the conveyor belt to get checked out and grabbed her bank card to pay.

"Well, we can do another dinner next time. Tell Stuart Jr. I'll talk to Christian about him coming over for a sleepover."

The cashier bagged up her groceries, and Teagan hung up with Sasha and grabbed them. She approached her car, unlocked the trunk, and placed three bags inside. She glanced up and saw the same woman who was staring at her in the store sitting in a car near the exit. Teagan held her hand up to block the sun and focus on the car the woman was driving. She tried to pull her phone out of her pocket to take a picture, but it was too late. The car sped off quickly. Teagan shook off the feeling and drove home to start dinner for her family for the first time since she went back to work full time.

Forty minutes later, she pulled into her driveway, turned the car off, and stared at her house. It seemed like a foreign concept to be back into the routine of wife and mother while the world turned without knowing the enemies she faced every time she left the house. The front door opened, and she saw her mother-in-law and Cole coming out to help her with the bags.

"Hi, Claudia." Teagan reached over to give her a hug.

"Hey, baby. You need help?" Claudia pulled back as Teagan popped the trunk, and she grabbed a bag. Cole tried to climb inside to get a bag, but he was too short.

"Hold Mommy's keys for me," Teagan told him, and he ran toward the front door excitedly.

"That boy is always trying to get into something."

Teagan followed her mother-in-law in the house and saw her two kids sitting on the floor in front of Christian, showing him their new toys. Christian came from the kitchen and helped to grab the bags out of their hands and kissed Teagan on the lips.

"Did you talk to Sasha?" Christian asked as he helped put the food away.

"I did. She wants to get together with the kids." Teagan opened the cabinet and pulled out a pan. Claudia washed her hands and grabbed the pan from her to help get dinner started. Teagan removed her jacket, lifted the apron from the back of the pantry door, and opened the fridge to grab some ingredients to start the sauce.

"CJ asked me about Stuart coming over, and I wanted to check with you first."

"I'll be here." Teagan set the temperature on the stove and prepared the food as her husband went back into the living room with the kids and his father.

"How are things going, Teagan?" Claudia smiled and grabbed the ingredients for the meat.

"Everything is fine."

"Christian's been worried about you, and the kids are hanging out at our house more than usual," Claudia mentioned. Teagan released a sigh, thinking of a way to approach the conversation without pushing her mother-in-law away. They'd never had a problem communicating with each other about the way the kids were being raised. Neither of them knew about her working for the government besides being retired from the Navy. If it came out about her being deep within the government, it could put a target on their backs. She and Christian made a promise to never get caught off guard. Since being home, the security system was upgraded from the inside and outside with cameras in different parts of the house. The president thought it would be a good idea to have security detail for the family, but Teagan declined, not wanting to scare the kids. Bad enough she had to leave them for assignments for long periods of time, but having guards surrounding their house at all hours of the night only brought on more questions and tension within the family.

"I know, and we talked about our work schedules. Things are smoothing out for us," Teagan replied. To her surprise, Claudia dropped the conversation and worked on cutting up the onions and tomatoes for the sauce. An hour later, they all sat around the table listening to Tatum talk about a new doll she wanted her parents to buy.

"Grandpa, can you please tell Daddy to buy the doll?" Tatum scooped some mashed potatoes together. Everyone at the table laughed at her question, while Teagan helped Cole to cut up portions of his steak.

"Did you finalize that deal for the software?" her father-in-law asked Christian.

"What deal?" Teagan asked, peering over at Christian.

"At the office, a new software concept I've been working on might get sold," Christian replied.

"For twenty million dollars," Claudia spoke, and Teagan's eyes widened in surprise.

"Oh, Daddy, that means I can buy a lot of dolls!" Tatum excitedly clapped her hands, standing on the chair. Teagan tickled Tatum on her stomach and kissed the side of her cheek as Christian walked to the kitchen with his plate. A few seconds later, he came back with her cell phone vibrating with a text message. At the same time, Claudia gasped and pointed at the TV.

"OMG!" Claudia tapped Christian on the shoulder to turn it up.

"We have breaking news. An attempted hacking at the defense department has been uncovered," Margaret from Channel Seven News said.

"What is going on in the world?" Claudia stood in shock.

Spider: You see the news?

Teagan: What's going on?

Spider: We think it has to do with Fenton.

Teagan: Who are we?

Spider: Gregory is still researching, but he did come across something.

Teagan: What?

Spider: The firm that created the software.

Teagan: Who is it?

Spider: Christian's company.

Teagan's phone slipped out of her hand as she glanced over at her husband.

"What's wrong?" Christian walked toward her, and she waved him off.

She broke eye contact and glanced around the room at her kids and in laws as they watched the TV play in the background.

"What's wrong, Teagan?" Claudia inquired.

Teagan took a gulp and bent down to pick up her phone as it rang with Spider's name across.

"Hello," Teagan muttered as she marched into the kitchen, standing in front of the sink, trying to control her vomit from rising. Once again, things were getting too close to home, and she would be in a position of having to choose between her family and saving the country.

"I have Gregory looking into it, but we need you to come back to the office," Spider rushed out. Teagan looked over her shoulder as Christian stepped in the kitchen and waited for her to end the call.

"I'll be there soon." Teagan ended the call and slid the phone in her pocket. Christian came up behind her and wrapped his arms around her waist.

"You have to go?"

Teagan nodded, turning around.

"Security Analyst Services."

"What about them?"

"How deep are you in on the building of the software?"

"Wait, hold up… You think I did this?" Christian motioned with his hands up.

"No, but I need to know everything you did."

"I built the software component, but it's not fully ready to be sold." Christian explained, standing across from her.

Teagan sighed, rubbing her temples.

"I need to go."

"Talk to me, Teagan."

"That was Spider. It's something about your company's software possibly being used for this hacking situation."

Christian's mouth dropped open in surprise.

"I'm going with you."

Teagan placed her hand against his chest, shaking her head side to side.

"I need you to stay here with the kids. Remember we agreed to let SJ come over, and I don't want to disappoint the kids."

Christian blew out a breath and ran a hand down his face.

"You're right. At least keep me updated if you need anything." Christian leaned over to peck her on the lips. Teagan hugged him and strolled out of the kitchen to the dining room to kiss the kids. She hugged Claudia and Chris goodbye as she grabbed her coat and purse to leave, still wearing her pantsuit from earlier.

Chapter Seven

Teagan scanned her ID through the security checkpoint of the building, walked through the metal detectors, and rode the escalator up to the main floor of their department. She didn't have the luxury as the director to bypass any special treatment; she was the one to enforce that no matter what. All clearance needed to be triple checked. The twenty-five-story building was made of steel, with the outside looking like a closed-off financial office. Inside it was a fully functioning, high-tech, modern office structure with top-of-the-line equipment specific to their needs. When it was time to build, Stanton wanted a gym, shooting range, cafeteria, and medic department onsite. On top of jail cells for criminals when they needed to bring people in for questioning. Teagan headed down the hall as people ran around in a panic over the breaking news. She wondered if the president was waiting to be briefed on any updates. Not only were they handling the Hernandez situation, now this had set off a chain of events. Teagan pushed the door of the strategy room open and saw Gregory and Broderick going back and forth. Daughtrey sat in a chair with a headset on, talking to someone.

"What do you have for me?" Teagan approached Gregory.

"SAS is still not online, and they're trying to figure out what happened." Gregory rolled his eyes at the lack of urgency from the owner not returning his call.

"Have you talked to their tech support?"

"That's the fun part; he's on vacation," Broderick chortled and crossed his arms over his chest.

"Your husband is at the company, right?" Gregory asked.

"Yeah, but I'm not dragging him into this mess."

"If it could help us, we should talk to him," Broderick mentioned.

"No."

"Teagan, you act like he doesn't know what you do. We would be discreet and let you handle the questioning," Broderick explained.

Teagan's head turned fast at Broderick in a scowl.

"Get the information on the tech support guy and bring him here now," Teagan demanded, holding onto the last little bit of nerves she had left. No one could understand that she was flying by on lack of sleep, little food, and the fear of bringing her husband into questioning that always ended with the suspect not leaving.

Broderick stalked off in a huff as Spider motioned for her at the door.

"He's been on edge since this started. Ignore him." Spider handed papers to Teagan who scanned over them; they all were numbers with longitude and latitude sequences.

"Did you break this yet?" Teagan asked, heading to her office with Spider behind her.

"I think this is Fenton's doing. It's escalating."

After Teagan scanned her handprint on the wall security screen, she went to sit at her desk and dialed the president on a secure line.

"Do we have any phone records of Fenton today before this happened?"

"I have Daughtrey checking now. I think we need to move now and not wait," Spider replied, as the phone was answered.

"Tell me I'm not seeing what I think I'm seeing, Director Stone."

Teagan had the phone on speaker.

"Mr. President, I'm afraid they've taken the first steps. We didn't anticipate this happening so fast."

"How is this even possible? Department of Defense!" President Sanders shouted.

"Yes, sir. I have my men working on finding the tech analyst who launched the software."

"When did this software get built?" the president asked.

Teagan looked over at Spider. Her palms were sweaty, and her head ached from having to involve her husband.

"I'm still looking into that, Mr. President," Teagan responded.

"Get on it, Agent Stone. You wanted this position, and now you have it. I want answers within the next thirty minutes," the president demanded, ending the call.

"Don't say it." Teagan sat back in her seat, staring up at the ceiling.

"He's not the only one who's looking for Christian," Spider stated.

"I know. Broderick already tried to talk me into bringing him in here."

"It's only a few news stations, but more than likely, the owner is going to throw Christian out to the sharks as the reason for the hack," Spider stated.

"We need to get to Fenton and Hernandez now."

"What are you thinking?"

"We got the secretary of defense to make a statement that everything is under control, and it wasn't a major breach. We need to keep Fenton from thinking we're on to him."

Gregory burst through the door. "I got something." He passed Teagan a small recording device and set the tape recorder in front of her desk and hit play.

Unknown: Everything is a go, Ramirez.

Ramirez: I want my money first.

"That's Fenton." Teagan sat up straight to hear.

Fenton: Check your account now.

Ramirez: If this falls back on me, I'm not covering for you.

Fenton: You just best make sure I have the right information.

Ramirez: I could go to jail for passing along classified information.

Fenton: Too late to have a heart now.

Some rustling on the line, then silence as the sound of typing was heard.

Ramirez: It's done.

Fenton: How long will it take?

Ramirez: Not long. As we speak, everyone is going to be freaking out about the security breach, and I'm heading out of the country.

Fenton: Good, make sure nothing traces back to me. You'll get the other half after Hernandez takes office.

Ramirez: Hey, that wasn't part of the plan.

Fenton: It is now.

Ambassador Fenton ended the call as Ramirez shouted and cursed about getting screwed over. Gregory placed a file folder on her desk and flipped it open.

"Ramirez Gusto, a ten-year tech analyst for SAS and recently retired," Gregory explained.

"Family?"

"Divorced with no kids, a mom who lives in Florida after retiring," Gregory said.

Teagan bit on her bottom lip, staring at Ramirez's employee file.

"I know what you're thinking, but there's another way." Spider sat on the edge of her desk.

"No."

"Teagan, we can't fly into Florida and strap his mom on a table to interrogate her son. It would be easier to talk with Christian about the software and possibly how to find Ramirez," Spider stated, watching the creases in her forehead disappear.

"I want someone on his mother and have someone get Christian to come in here."

"On it," Gregory said, walking off.

"Gregory, tell him I sent for him and make sure nothing happens to him," Teagan muttered, picking up the photos of Ramirez again. Oval-shaped face with bushy brows, thick lips, narrow nose. Bald head and standing around five-seven. No kids or wife, with a gambling debt of sixty thousand dollars to loan sharks.

"Don't worry, we have all the airports alerted." Spider stood from the desk.

"If this recording was done in the last thirty minutes or more, he's probably not taking a flight straightaway," Teagan said.

"We can get people on the bus stations."

"I want him broadcasted on the news."

"What if we cause Fenton to run?" Spider questioned.

"Get a flight back to Spain. Fenton won't run. Everything resides on Hernandez being the next prime minister."

"I hope you know what you're doing, Teagan."

"Me too," Teagan mumbled under her breath as Spider walked out of her office. She turned in her chair and stared at a family photo of the kids with Christian at Disneyland a few years back. A knock at her door pulled her out of her daze.

"Come in," she called out.

"They're pulling in with Christian now," Gregory stated, and Teagan got out of her chair.

"Bring him to my office and get Spider."

"Do you want the rest of the team here?"

"No. Keep working on finding Ramirez and get the president updated." Teagan watched as her husband came into her office. He glanced around the room that he'd never seen before. Any time she left for work, he pictured her sitting in some cubicle getting updates and talking with her Navy friends about old times.

"Christian, have a seat." Teagan motioned to the chair in front of her desk.

"I've never been to your office."

"I know it's strange, but being the director, I have to be formal."

"You look good in that role. I never had the chance to congratulate you," Christian complimented.

"Thank you, but if it weren't for Stanton betraying The Firm, I wouldn't be in the position."

"What position is that?"

"Talking to you."

"About the software."

Teagan nodded, came around the front of her desk, and stood next to him.

"What can you tell me about Ramirez Gusto?"

"He's behind this?"

"I can't answer that."

"But you think he is; otherwise, I wouldn't be here."

"Did he ever complain to you or anyone at work about being unhappy?" Teagan asked.

"I didn't talk to him much. I only created the software and trained the analysts on how it worked."

"Would you be able to read out the numbers?"

"Probably, but it depends on if he used the same coding setup."

Teagan leaned behind herself and grabbed the printout that Gregory gave her earlier.

"Tell me what you see."

Christian took it out of her hands and scanned over the document. She watched his eyes narrow in confusion.

"This isn't what I wrote up." Christian handed the papers back to Teagan.

"What do you mean?"

"Whatever he was doing not only can destroy the department, but it can be used for other government agencies. It needs to be shut down because the codes give off timestamps that can be triggered from anywhere."

"Can you do it?"

"Maybe."

Teagan pushed the call center button on her phone.

"Still working on Ramirez," Gregory spoke.

"Have someone handle that. Partner with Christian on overriding the database."

"Sounds good."

Christian stood, turned Teagan's chin toward him, caressed her cheek, and stared into her eyes.

"You need to rest."

"Once this case is over, I will."

"I take it you're not coming home with me tonight."

"I'm flying out to Spain."

Christian groaned, and she grasped his palm in her hand.

"I promise a vacation just you and the kids once everything is over."

"Can you promise to be safe?" Christian questioned. Teagan dropped his hand.

"You know I can't make that promise."

"Then don't give me false hope, Teagan."

The door opened, and Spider walked in with a smile on his face.

"Hey, Christian."

"Hey."

"Gregory is waiting on you outside the door."

Spider stood in the middle of the floor, feeling the tension between Teagan and Christian as they stared at each other.

"Call me and let me know when you're safe," Christian said.

"I will," Teagan replied, knowing she wasn't coming home tonight. The unwritten rule in their marriage had always been about a shared love of independence. Neither wanted to hold the other back, but Christian, deep down, was growing more and more frustrated that her job overshadowed their family.

"Our plane leaves in two hours."

"Okay, let me call the president and update him. Then we can load up the van to get going."

"Hey, are you all right?"

"Yeah. Why do you ask?"

"If you want to stay, Teagan, it's okay not to take the lead on this mission," Spider told.

"And have Broderick in control?"

"There are other people we could use."

"I'll be fine. Go check on Christian." She waved him off, picked up the phone, and dialed the secure line for the president. She closed her eyes while thinking how her life had changed.

Chapter Eight

A week later.

The team arrived back in Spain a day earlier and went to the home of their contact Acevedo Vasquez, current military on the prime minister's security detail. He was unmarried, with no kids. He helped to tip off the president about what Fenton and Hernandez were trying to pull off. A map laid on the table as they all stood around and went over the details of the crowd and security he had established.

"Fenton's going to be there. If he sees us," Teagan spoke.

"I know, which is why I think you should dress in our uniform," Acevedo answered.

"The news is going to be all over this. How do we get him before they swear him in?" Spider questioned.

"We have a short window of time," Broderick said.

"Acevedo will let us in the room?"

"The second we contact him. Things should run through here," Spider said, pointed to the area around Zarzuela Palace.

"How long are you thinking?" Teagan asked Acevedo.

"It shouldn't be more than thirty minutes to take him," Acevedo replied.

"Once we take him, what do we do?" Gregory stated.

"Kill him," Teagan remarked.

"That will start an international crime," Broderick said.

"The president wants the ambassador arrested, and Hernandez accidentally dies in an accident," Teagan explained, circling Hernandez and Fenton's photos.

"Who takes over?" Spider inquired, putting on his bulletproof vest and military uniform.

"Someone the president has worked with and wants to support the country's policies."

"Who?" Spider and Broderick asked at the same time.

"Me," Acevedo replied.

"So, we're going beyond The Firm's reach?" Daughtrey said, running a hand down his face.

"Hernandez has too much power. The second he takes the oath of office, it's over," Teagan explained, tying her boots.

"We have no choice. The president made the call." After Teagan slid her jacket on, she grabbed an extra gun and put it in her holster.

"Are you ready to take over and govern a country? I mean, are they going to accept him?" Spider questioned, peering at Acevedo. He followed Teagan as she carried two bags outside.

"He's ready to take over, and Acevedo is popular in Spain. His campaign will have the full backing of the US," Teagan explained, loading up the black Hummer.

"Daughtrey, you're driving the second car; it's bulletproof. Broderick, you're with Acevedo and me," Teagan told them, opening the passenger door and putting on her seatbelt.

Removing everything that could incriminate them, Gregory walked out with the map, so they'd be prepared.

Spider passed Teagan a walkie and an earpiece, so they'd all stay in contact. Acevedo passed Teagan the latest Hernandez photo with him walking off the plane and getting inside the limo to head to the swearing-in ceremony.

"Make sure you try to avoid any gunfire as much as possible," Teagan remarked over the walkie.

"Copy that," Gregory said.

The car started with Acevedo driving, and Broderick in the backseat. It was going on ten in the morning, and normally, they'd do operations at night, thus not having to shield themselves so much. Teagan thought of every scenario that could cause a ripple in the plan. It was the only way for her to stay on top of things and not get distracted by stressing about her family. Daughtrey continued heading toward the location of the swearing-in ceremony, past the embassy.

Thirty minutes later, the team pulled up to the palace's back, a few blocks from the security checkpoint. Dressed in the appropriate gear, they'd be able to infiltrate without having any questions come upon them to hold up the mission. Daughtrey parked and pulled the key out of the ignition as Teagan turned to look at everyone.

"Daughtrey, you ditch the car and get us something else while we go in to grab him," Teagan spoke.

"What's the official plan?" Acevedo questioned.

"We switch him out with you and go underground," Spider replied, nodding at Teagan. He cocked his gun back and slid the shades on, before stepping out of the car, followed by everybody else. They mixed in with the crowd of guards as they lined up, ready to go through the checkpoint to receive the assignment. As the plans came together, they placed a trustworthy person on Hernandez's team to allow them inside without any questions. Teagan and Spider stood with Acevedo next to them, wearing shades. They were waved to step forward through the pat down.

"Room 215," the guard spoke to Acevedo. He looked up at the building, noticing the guards standing in unison. He focused on the growing crowds of people wearing shirts with Hernandez's face and cheering in support for his confirmation. Teagan came up behind him, motioning with the tip of her nose to move forward up the side stairs through the guards. Keeping her earpiece in, she checked every angle of the snipers' location to keep in mind as they drew closer to get their suspect.

"Room 215," Acevedo repeated Teagan.

The front steps of the palace doors opened as Hernandez was escorted out to greet the crowd, surrounded by a few agents. In Teagan's mind, it was the perfect opportunity. She scanned the crowd as the cheers heightened and made eye contact with Spider and Acevedo. It was time. Spider slid next to Acevedo, with Teagan on the right side. They walked toward Hernandez as he came down a few stairs and waved at the people. Teagan slipped her hand in her pocket, tightened her hand around the cell, pushed the number button for one, and an explosion of confetti startled the guards, but the citizens loved the massive display. Hernandez smiled, giving the thumb's up in excitement, and pointed toward the flying banner with his name inscribed. His men clapped and cheered, not paying attention as Teagan came up the side of him and accidentally tripped Hernandez with her left foot. He tumbled to the ground, but no one paid attention as Spider came up beside Hernandez and pretended to help him up. He slipped a syringe into him next, covered his eyes with a pair of shades while helping him to stand. Acevedo stood in front of him without his shades or hat on, dressed exactly like Hernandez. Both had the same hair, eye color, and skin tone. Teagan and Spider picked Hernandez up from the ground and carried him to the side of the wall with his head down as Acevedo continued pretending to be Hernandez.

"Hernandez! Hernandez!" the crowd on the streets shouted. A few seconds went by, and Teagan set off another round of confetti and motioned for Spider to go ahead down the steps. He put his arms around his shoulders, and his head stayed down. Some guards laughed as he stumbled through the throng of people.

"Daughtrey, what do you have for us?" Teagan said into her

earpiece, looking over her shoulder as she stayed a few feet behind Spider.

"The north corner, I have another year," Daughtrey mentioned.

Teagan and Spider caught up with the rest of the team and went through the side door of a local cafe one block from the palace. They marched through the back entrance as a group of people watched the coronation on a TV that hung on the wall. Spider busted through the backdoor off the alleyway, still holding onto Hernandez as he groaned.

"Keep him quiet," Teagan whispered.

"What do you want to do about the swearing in?" Broderick stated. Teagan opened the door that led to the train station on the north corner. He noticed it wasn't as crowded with the events going on across town at the palace. People moved out of their way as they stalked across the walkway just in time for the train to arrive. The doors opened for everyone to come and go. The team took Hernandez over to the bathroom and checked to make sure no one was inside.

"Get him changed," Teagan stated, standing outside the door. Spider and Broderick lifted a bag out of the trash can, and a janitor's uniform was inside for everyone. Teagan set her watch for five minutes and waited for them to stroll out as people tried to use the bathroom.

"Out of order, sorry," Teagan said to the group of teenage boys.

They nodded and walked out, whispering about her. The guys unlocked the doors and stepped out with Hernandez still knocked out and wearing an orange janitor jumpsuit.

"You have two minutes to change." Broderick handed her a jumpsuit, and Teagan went into the stall and wiped away any sign of being in the Army. She opened the door as her cell vibrated. Lifting it in her hand, she saw a message.

"*It's done.*" President Sanders sent an attachment of Acevedo being sworn in as Fenton stood to the side with a smile on his face.

"Heading back now," Teagan typed back. All the clothes were tossed back in the trash can with lighter fluid poured on top. Broderick lit a match, causing the train to be evacuated.

"Let's go," Broderick said, and Teagan checked the time and lightly jogged behind them down the hall to the other end of the train station. The crew jumped down onto the tracks while police shouted for people to get back as they tried to contain the fire. Spider and Broderick pushed Hernandez up against the wall as they came to a stop in front of a door. Teagan popped the lock to let them inside. As they walked through, she looked forward while Broderick looked backwards. She came upon the end of the trail and saw stairs hanging down. She climbed up to see if the signal would give better direction. Teagan pushed the pothole up slowly.

"What do you see?" Spider questioned.

"It's clear." Teagan looked around and saw an empty street. She climbed out and waited for Spider to come up next.

"Daughtrey was clear," Teagan spoke into the walkie.

A few seconds later, a blue janitorial workers' van came around the corner and eased up beside the team. The door opened with Daughtrey stepping out to help pull Hernandez up. Teagan scanned the street from left to right.

"One minute, guys," Teagan said.

"He's fucking heavy, man," Broderick complained and tossed Hernandez in the back and checked his vitals. Teagan jumped in the front seat as Daughtrey closed the pothole and sealed it back up with the tools from the van.

"Is the plan ready?" Broderick asked.

Teagan grabbed her phone from her pocket.

"Mr. President, we have the package," Teagan said.

"Good, make sure we have no problems from here on out," the president replied.

Teagan ended the call, put the phone back in her pocket, and grabbed her gun out of her holster.

"Plan still on track?" Spider looked at her, and she motioned for Daughtrey to take the next street to the left as they drove away to a secure location.

Teagan stared out of the side mirror as cars passed. She ignored his question until a police car blaring its sirens drove past them in the opposite direction.

Chapter Nine

"Now, it is," Teagan said and pulled her phone out of her pocket.

"This wasn't supposed to happen," a voice said over the phone.

"Mr. Prime Minister, what are you speaking about?" she asked.

"Fenton, he's dead," Prime Minister Castillo said.

Teagan looked over her shoulder and winked at Spider.

"I assure you, Mr. Prime Minister. We had nothing to do with Ambassador Fenton," Teagan stated.

"The president promised to keep this clean," Castillo whispered over the phone.

"He did, but I didn't." Teagan hung up the phone and tossed it out the window. The van drove for another fifteen minutes until they came to a private airport and parked. The doors opened, and Teagan jumped out, helping to grab the bags and pass them to the crew to carry onboard.

"What did you do?" Spider questioned, crossing his arms over his chest.

"I did my job," Teagan said.

"What are you talking about?" Broderick inquired.

"Fenton is no longer with us. If you have a problem with my decision, I suggest you speak now."

"Does the president know?" Broderick questioned.

"He will now when it airs across the news," Teagan told me.

"We need to get out of here before he wakes." Spider pointed to Hernandez being dragged on the plane. All three stepped on as Daughtrey pushed smelling salt underneath Hernandez's nose to wake him.

"Mmmmm..." Hernandez mumbled.

"Mr. Hernandez, I'm Agent Red, and you're under arrest." Teagan maneuvered around Hernandez, glanced around the plane, and saw everybody staring back at him.

"Who are you?" he groggily asked, trying to lift his hand, but got cut off by a pair of handcuffs around his wrist and the seat.

"Doesn't matter. What's about to happen to you is the most important," Teagan replied and motioned for Daughtrey to knock him out again. Teagan went to sit near the back of the plane with Spider following.

Over seven hours later, the plane arrived back in New York, and four black SUVs sat on the tarmac for them to load up and head to the office. Teagan stepped down the stairs and marched to the first SUV as her cell phone rang.

"Agent Stone."

"Stone? Teagan Stone, director of The Firm?" the voice asked.

Teagan squinted her eyes and pulled the phone away from her face.

"Who is this?"

"Mrs. Stone, this is Abe Price of National News."

"Director Stone to you."

"My apologies."

"How can I help you, Mr. Price?"

"I'd like to speak with you about the situation with the Department of Defense being hacked," Abe spoke.

"I'm not the person to ask about that."

"According to my sources, a Christian Hawkins was the creator of the software, and he happens to be married to you, the director of The Firm, a well-known government agency."

Teagan lifted her index finger to her mouth for Spider to be quiet.

"Mr. Price, whatever you're thinking, I suggest you rethink what you plan to write."

"Have your memories come back fully?" he inquired.

"What are you trying to do?" Teagan turned in her seat to look out the back window at the other cars trailing. The driver started the car and drove off into traffic back to the city.

"I'm just doing my job," Abe explained.

"Well, Mr. Price, I have no comment for your story."

"Is that your final answer?"

Teagan's face twitched.

"Is there something you want to ask me?"

"How is it possible for you to come back into the role without any type of confirmation from Congress? Why is The Firm still around? It's well documented the amount of torture and killing that takes place on the word of the president."

Teagan gritted her teeth.

"Mr. Price, I don't know what you're talking about. The government doesn't torture detainees."

"On the record."

"How did you sleep last night?"

"What?"

"I asked, how did you sleep last night?"

"Fine, I guess," Abe replied. Teagan ended the call and tossed the phone out the window.

"Then we did our job right." The second SUV rode over the phone, crushing it to pieces.

"Who was that?" Spider questioned.

"Nobody."

Spider slid his hand in his pocket, removed his phone, and made a call.

"Gregory ordered another cell phone for Teagan. It fell out of the window," Spider commented, glancing at Teagan as she stared out the window.

"Any updates on Acevedo?" Teagan questioned.

"He's reversed some of the plans Matias had in place. It's already spread about Fenton."

"Soon as we get information from Matias, we can inform the president."

"What do you plan to do with Hernandez?

"I'm going to have a conversation with him."

"If he doesn't talk?"

"He will."

The gate opened at the garage for all four cars to pull in and line up next to each other. Security detail removed the license plates and unloaded the bags. Hernandez was still out cold when Gregory and Daughtrey picked him up.

"Take him to the room," Teagan said, removing her jacket and rubbing the back of her neck. The team split with Gregory and Daughtrey headed to the interrogation room, and Teagan, Spider, and Broderick going to the conference room. They stepped on the elevator and hit the button for the restricted-access basements.

"Have you talked to Christian?" Spider inquired.

Teagan wondered if Abe had contacted Christian about the hacking situation since she hadn't spoken with him since being undercover on this mission.

"Not yet. I need to call him and check in on the kids." All three stepped off the elevator and walked down the dark hallway. It brought back memories of when she was held captive.

"We can take the lead on the questioning," Broderick said.

"I don't doubt that, Broderick, but we're already on high alert in the media."

Broderick scanned his hand on the monitor, followed by Spider and Teagan, and the black steel door opened. The room was a replica of when she sat in the same spot, answering questions about who she was and what she'd done in her time in the Navy. Two-way mirrors displayed Hernandez on the other side with his head down. Daughtrey and Gregory stood next to him.

"You remember your first time doing this?" Broderick asked. Teagan peered at the mirror in thought.

Flashback nine years ago.

Teagan paced back and forth in front of double agent Dillion Houston, a former operative of the agency who sold their secrets to the Russian government. A young Teagan, fresh out of training, was working her first case as a spy.

"Dillion, would you like something to drink?" Teagan questioned.

Dillion sat back in the chair with his arms crossed and a smug grin on his face.

"You think I'm stupid?" Dillion chuckled, sliding his hand through his short, blond hair. Greenish brown eyes glanced at the door, then back at Teagan, possibly thinking of how he could escape after killing her. Everyone took Teagan's size and height as a disadvantage, but she knew what she could do to someone if they tried to attack. Training in the Navy alongside men who she thought of as brothers taught her to always be on the go if someone even thought of testing her. For example, she removed his handcuffs from his wrists and offered him something to drink to try to gain his trust. But she wasn't a fool; she had men on the other side of the door waiting in case he tried anything.

"I think you're scared."

"You think you're better than me? I did what I had to do."

Teagan snorted with derision.

"What do you mean?" Teagan went to sit down in the chair opposite him and clasped her hands together.

"Stanton's not to be trusted; he's the one who should be brought up on charges, not me."

"Stanton's our boss, Dillion. What do you think he's done exactly?"

Dillion waved her off.

"You're just like them."

Teagan slammed her hand on the table.

"I'm trying to help you. My men out there right now want to torture you or even worse, kill you!"

"You can't save me!" Dillion yelled.

Teagan saw a spark in his eye for a split second of fearing the outcome. Using her college psych classes, she cleared her throat and sat forward in the chair.

"I spoke with your parents."

Dillion grunted and jumped up in his seat, pointing a finger in her face as the doors burst open, and two soldiers charged toward him.

"Leave my family out of this, bitch!" Dillion tried to grab her arm, and she bent his wrist back and twisted his arm.

"No, it's all right. Let him go."

"Are you sure?" the soldier asked.

"Dillion, are you ready to sit and talk like an adult?"

Dillion jerked out of the hold he was in and sat back down, his face drawn up in a scowl with an evil smile.

"I'm not saying a word without a lawyer."

"Too bad, because in the agency, you're one phone call is me."

Teagan motioned for the soldiers to take him away, and he screamed, knowing where he was being taken.

"Wait! I... I... talk," Dillion screamed.

"Too late; this bitch is no longer in the mood."

Teagan stood at the door as they escorted him down the hallway to the chamber. All detainees were put there if they didn't cooperate.

Chapter Ten

Present.

Teagan went to answer a knock at the door, and an employee held out a cell phone for her to take.

"Thanks."

"What's the plan?"

Teagan sighed and watched as Hernandez finally looked up and focused on the mirror in front of him. All through training when she was younger, she witnessed many men and some women who died from certain techniques, and she promised herself that if she were in charge, those tactics wouldn't be sanctioned under her watch. Trusting herself to follow through was the one question she had to ask herself because this wouldn't be the last man she would have to deal with who came between the safety of the American people.

"Broderick go in and talk with him first. I want to see how he takes it to you."

"I thought you didn't want me."

Teagan waved her hand.

"Realistically, I shouldn't, but you two have something in common that I can use."

"What's that?"

"Your hatred for me," Teagan responded and leaned against the wall as Broderick nodded and walked out of the room.

"How much longer are you going to keep him on the team?" Spider stood next to her, focusing on Hernandez as Broderick walked inside and took a seat.

"I don't trust him, but I like to keep my enemies close."

Teagan hit the intercom on the wall and listened to the conversation.

"Hernandez, we have reason to believe you were working with Ambassador Fenton to infiltrate our government," Broderick said.

"I don't know anything about that."

"You do know Ambassador Fenton, correct?"

"Yes, of course."

"How much was he paying you?"

"I don't know what you're talking about?"

"You can be honest with me. We're all friends here. I was in your shoes once."

"What do you mean by that?" Hernandez held his hands in his lap.

"Feeling like I knew what was best for my country to making decisions to get rid of the people who tried to come between what I thought was best." Broderick peered over his shoulder, and Teagan caught his message.

"That woman, is she in charge?" Hernandez questioned.

"Agent Stone and I have different points of view on certain things, namely you." Broderick pointed at Hernandez.

"I had nothing to do with Fenton or some cover up," Hernandez spat.

"Then tell us what the plan was."

"I need to speak with the president."

Teagan pushed the intercom button.

"Mr. Castillo, the president isn't taking calls from traitors of one's own country," Teagan stated.

Hernandez's eyes rose in fear.

"I want to speak with Fenton. This is all a misunderstanding," Hernandez said.

"He's not available," Broderick responded.

As Broderick continued trying to get answers from him, Teagan's cell phone rang. She answered and stepped into the hallway.

"Mr. President, we have Hernandez."

"I got a message that Abe Price tried to reach out to you about the hack of the Department of Defense," the president said.

"He called when our plane landed."

"Did you ever find Ramirez?"

"Not yet, sir."

"This could become a problem, Agent Stone, that we don't need."

"I understand, sir, but I'm handling it as we speak."

"I know that Christian is caught up in this, and Abe is looking for a scapegoat."

"He can try, but I'm not falling for his game."

"Is Matias talking?"

"No, but I'm only observing for now."

"We don't need any more bad press on this. Get him into custody if you have to and bring him up on charges."

"Mr. President, giving him the choice to even think he could get away with this is bad and sets us up for all our enemies."

"What do you suggest? We have one dead ambassador, a missing tech analyst, and your husband in the news for possibly working with terrorists," the president remarked.

"Give me more time, sir."

"You have twenty-four hours, Agent, before I shut this down," President Sanders ended the call, and Teagan rubbed her temples in frustration. She walked into the interrogation room and slammed the door. She pushed the phone in her pocket, walked up on Matias, and gripped the back of his neck, slamming him down on the floor with her foot on his neck.

"I have twenty-four hours to do anything I want, and that includes making you disappear off the face of the earth."

"Please. I didn't do anything," Matias whimpered.

"I suggest you tell me everything. Where's Ramirez Gusto?"

A tear pulled into his eyes, and Teagan put more pressure on his neck, then removed her foot and helped him to sit up in the chair. Hernandez tried to catch his breath, and Teagan motioned for them to bring him water.

"Matias, this only goes one way, and that's you living in prison for the rest of your life."

Gregory brought him a bottle of water, and he gulped it down.

"This was all Fenton's idea. I didn't know how far he would go."

"We saw the photos of you two, Matias. Please don't speak to me like I'm stupid."

"He planned this all out from the beginning. He was in debt and was promised millions of dollars if we worked together," Matias replied.

"Then what? From what I saw, you were equal partners in trying to pass deals that would put a lot of money in your hands and destroy our country."

"Ramirez was Fenton's guy. He brought him in, and I refused him at first, but Fenton was pushy."

"Where's Ramirez?" Broderick questioned.

"All I knew was the number to send the second half of the money," Matias replied.

"Tell me the number." Teagan pulled out her phone.

"Browser Banking 345-695-9896-90," Matias responded.

"Gregory, get as much information as you can."

"You got it."

"Do you have any type of phone number for Ramirez?" Teagan questioned.

"No. Fenton handled all that," Matias said.

"Trace his phone records, Gregory," Teagan ordered.

Gregory nodded and walked out of the room.

"Daughtrey, take him to the cell for now. President Sanders wants us to wait while the media attention is high."

Teagan turned and headed to the door.

"Am I going to live, Agent Red?" Matias said, calling her out by name. Teagan slowly released her hand from the knob of the door and glanced over her shoulder.

"Would you release a traitor of your country?" Teagan asked. Matais shook his head left to right. Teagan walked out, leaving Daughtrey and Broderick with Matias.

Chapter Eleven

Two days later, Teagan was still in search of Ramirez, watching the entire media circus continue to implode about the missing tech analyst. After running his phone number and offshore account through databases, they had one option that came up as a potential lead. In Cuba, Ramirez was reported to be hiding out when the second part of his funds were cut off from being distributed. Spider and Teagan came up with a plan to send in their own intelligence agents to apprehend him while they worked on cleaning up the mess Fenton left behind.

Teagan turned the volume up on the TV in her office.

"This smells like a cover up to me, Jonathan," Sandra from Channel Seven News stated.

"No word from the White House about Ambassador Fenton," Jonathan replied.

"What are the odds of an attack on our technology and internet services? Plus, our ambassador to Spain is missing." Sandra looked into the camera.

"From what our sources say at National News, it's something to do with the creator of the software, Christian Hawkins," Jonathan said.

"Fuck!" Teagan blew out a breath and tossed the remote on her desk as Spider knocked on the door and stepped inside.

"You have to stop watching that crap. All those news shows are the same."

"They just named Christian now."

"Think it was that newspaper guy?"

"No one else knew."

"Need us to handle him?"

"No, that will only cause more problems. I'll talk with him. Did you get anything about Ramirez yet?"

Spider passed a file to Teagan, and she flipped it open, showing a dead Ramirez.

"What happened to him?" Teagan looked up at Spider.

"He returned fire."

"Is that the truth or something to make the president feel good to say to the media?"

"It wasn't my call, Teagan. Since it wasn't our own people, we couldn't demand the steps to bring him back to the States."

"That's bullshit, Spider."

"Look, I know you're under pressure, but you have to make these calls, or other people will make them for you."

"I wanted to be different. We can't go around killing people." Teagan jumped up and walked to the window in her office.

"Our jobs at the end of the day are to protect an oath we took."

"Even if that means destroying the foundation of what the country was built on?"

"Stanton wasn't all wrong."

"He was a traitor to the agency and blinded by greed."

"They're all like that, Teagan. You have blood on your hands just as much."

"I never asked for this!" Teagan waved her hand around.

"But you didn't turn it away either," Spider barked back.

"You've always told me the truth." Teagan turned and faced him.

"Are your memories slowly coming back?"

"Some. I remember my first interrogation with Dillion

Houston. Plus, meeting Diablo and pretending to be into Art," Teagan chortled.

"Call Christian and spend some time with your family."

"I will once this gets settled."

"You've done your job, Teagan. You no longer have to carry the burdens of your past."

"Why do I feel like this will never end?"

"Our lives are the agency; only you decided to strike out and have some sort of normalcy, but it never ends like that."

"I need to call this reporter."

"Be better than Stanton. Don't hide us."

"Why do you say that?"

"That causes more confusion and corruption. You don't have to say everything but own what we are and how we help," Spider spoke.

"Thanks, Spider."

He leaned over and gave her a hug.

Teagan walked back to her desk, blew out a breath, and picked up the phone.

"Abe Price, National News."

"Mr. Price, this is Teagan Stone."

Spider smirked and headed out of her office.

"I was waiting for you to call," Abe said.

"Are you watching Channel Seven News?" Teagan questioned.

"No, should I be?"

"You might find it interesting, or you could meet with me and get a better story."

"On the agency?" Abe said.

"Just meet me at Bronx Park in twenty minutes."

"Am I being detained? I do have family, Agent Stone, if I come up missing," Abe responded. Teagan laughed.

"Just be there if you want the scoop," Teagan said, ending the call.

Twenty minutes later, Teagan sat in the back of a black SUV, scoping out the area for any signs of trouble. Seeing one guy sitting on a bench that matched the file she pulled on Abe Price had her getting out of the car and heading toward him wearing her black trench coat. It was going on three in the afternoon, and she wanted to get back to work to finish filing away the case on Hernandez and Fenton.

"Mr. Price." Teagan sat on the same side as Abe to get a better view of all points of exit if she felt threatened.

"Agent Stone, or is it Red? Agent Red I like better." Abe smirked, holding his hand out for a shake.

"You've done your homework." Teagan reached out and shook his hand.

"Always, that's why they pay me the big bucks."

"I wanted to meet because things have escalated if you haven't noticed."

Abe pulled out a tape recorder.

"Off the record." Teagan took the recorder and put it in her pocket.

"Hey, come on, Agent Stone. I'm only doing my job."

"I understand, but if you want me to tell you what we do, I need some assurance it won't turn into an international incident."

"I promise to not focus on your husband within the story."

"He should be scrubbed off the entire article." Teagan glanced at the mom picking up her son and kissing him on the cheek.

"The basis of the software hinges on him."

"Doesn't matter. My family is not to be involved."

"What do I get out of this?"

"The former director of the agency was compromised and had an affair."

"I need more than that. Affairs nowadays don't cause an eyebrow to raise."

"The former ambassador of Spain was complicit in trying to cause a coup by the US government."

Abe's jaw dropped in shock.

"You must be kidding me. Fenton, right? I knew he was into some shit."

Teagan nodded and looked out over at the mother and two kids playing in the park, reminding her of what she had at home.

"Look into Stanton and Fenton, and you'll have your article" Teagan stood and started to walk away.

"Agent Stone!" Abe called out, and Teagan stopped and turned.

"Any truth to Matias Hernandez still being alive?" he asked.

"That's classified, Mr. Price." She held a neutral facial expression.

Teagan got back to the car as the driver started it up and slid the seatbelt on as she watched him write out notes.

"Back to the office, ma'am?" the driver asked.

"Yeah, I need to get ahead of things before he publishes the story."

Twenty minutes later, Teagan sat in her office with stacks of classified file boxes surrounding her desk. Spider knocked on the door and stepped inside, holding bags of food.

"I thought you'd be hungry, so I got you sandwiches from the cafeteria." Spider placed the two drinks down and passed the bag holding a turkey club sandwich over, sitting in the chair in front of her desk. Teagan thanked him, put the file down, and opened the bag of food.

"What are you expecting to find, Teagan? We both know that our jobs come with some degree of secrecy."

"I understand but have you ever wondered how this place was built?"

"I found some documents in the files about the Gulf War and Officer Abrahams." Teagan lifted the file and passed it toward Spider.

"What's this?" Spider flipped through the statements of each officer.

"Stanton's time in the CIA is in there and the death certificate they found at the market in Iraq."

"Do you know what this could do if it gets out to the public?" Spider closed the folder, tossed it on her desk, and jumped up.

"I've been grappling with that decision since I got back from speaking with Abe Price."

Spider stopped in front of the window.

"The guy from National News, Teagan!"

"I had to give him something, or he'd come after Christian," Teagan whispered back. The tension in the room was high as they glared at each other, both wanting to define their beliefs.

"Don't worry. I didn't give you up or the agency. More about Stanton and Hernandez."

"That could still backfire on us."

"I'll take the fall. I was the one who was recruited back into the agency against my will."

The phone rang on her desk, and she slowly picked it up, hesitant in who was on the other line.

"Agent Stone," Teagan said.

"Turn on Channel Seven News," the voice said and hung up.

Teagan picked up the remote and turned to Channel Seven as it showed breaking information.

"I have exclusive reporting that Ramirez Gusto, the man behind the attempted hacking, was found dead in Cuba." Sandra Gregg, news anchor of GNS reported.

"Teagan, does the president know about this?" Spider remarked.

"No, but I'll take the fall for everything to protect my family."

"From what I'm hearing, he was in Cuba, on the run. Also, I have information on someone named Stanton, a former director of a government spy agency," Sandra explained.

Teagan turned the TV off and sat in the chair. Her phone rang.

"That's him," Spider said.

"Mr. President."

Chapter Twelve

"Who leaked this information?" the president asked.

"It was me, sir."

"What was the reason for aligning with the press?"

"It was better if we controlled the narrative, sir. This way, he's more likely to come to us before snooping around behind our backs."

"Everything is going to be questioned now that Stanton's dead. They might even want to know what happened in Spain with Diablo."

"They won't."

President Sanders sighed on the other end of the call.

"The entire process of this agency was compromised before it even got started. We both know what Stanton and General Jones did in the past."

"I put you in this position because you wanted to clean things up. I didn't give you permission to throw us under the bus," President Sanders argued.

"If you want me to step down, I will. I never asked to be here!" Teagan yelled back.

"Abe Price is your responsibility. If anything goes wrong, I will personally hold you responsible," President Sanders demanded and ended the call.

Teagan grabbed her things, picked up the box with Abraham and Simpson's information, and left the office for the day. In the backseat of the SUV, she continued to look out the tinted window at people driving and talking along the streets with no clue or idea of the things she'd seen and done to keep them safe. For a brief few years, she lived in that bubble of the unknown with her memory of the time at war in the back of her mind. Now, she was back full force and commanding agents on what cases to take and covering up for certain individuals to protect their families.

"Have a good night, ma'am," the driver said.

"Thanks, Teddy. Take the rest of the day off. I'm in for the night."

"I know you're still trying to recapture your memories, but I appreciate you sticking to your guns," Teddy said.

Teagan smiled and grabbed the box, jacket, and her purse and pushed the door open to step out.

"Get home safe, Teddy." Teagan leaned back up from the passenger side window and turned to head in the house. Christian's car was in the driveway. Teagan put the key in the door and turned the knob to step into a quiet house with two of her kids sitting on the couch, watching a movie. Christian sat on the other end with papers in his hand. Teagan placed the box, jacket, and purse down on the floor next to the coat hanger.

"Hi, Mommy!" Cole and Tatum screamed, jumping up to give her a hug and kiss.

"Hi, were you two good for Daddy?" Teagan asked.

"Yes!" they both said.

Teagan kissed both their foreheads, and they walked back to the couch and cuddled under the blanket.

"You look tired." Christian put the papers down on the table and extended his hand for Teagan to take as she sat in his lap.

"Long day in the office."

"What did they do?"

"I'm taking care of it. Don't worry." Teagan kissed him on the lips.

"You hungry?" Christian questioned.

"No, I ate at the office." Teagan kicked off her heels and wrapped her arm around his neck.

Christian ran his hand up and down her back.

"Did your parents leave?" Teagan asked.

"Yeah, and they took CJ with them. He wanted to spend the night, so I said it was fine." The doorbell rang, and Teagan looked at Christian confused.

"Who could that be?" Teagan rose from his lap, went to the front door, and answered.

"Surprise!" Sasha and Stuart said at the same time, holding a bottle of wine.

"What are you doing here?" Sasha took the bottle of wine and handed it to Teagan. She stepped to the side to let them in with SJ behind them.

"Well, I know things were cancelled the other day. So, we decided to surprise you guys," Sasha stated and went toward the kids on the couch to hug them both.

"This is a surprise," Teagan mumbled to herself.

"Have a seat." Christian waved to the loveseat opposite him.

"Thanks," Stuart replied, removing his jacket.

A glance between Teagan and Christian was held for a split second. Sasha jumped up and entwined her arm with Teagan.

"So, tell me what happened. Is CJ all right?" Sasha questioned.

"What are you talking about?"

Christian cleared his throat.

"CJ's fine, Sasha. You remember, babe. He came down with a cold. That's why we canceled the sleepover," Christian told me.

"Ohh, yeah. That's right; he was sick. Caught something from another kid at school."

"Hopefully, my little nugget is good. Let's open a bottle of wine and catch up with the girl." Sasha grabbed the bottle off the table and stepped into the kitchen. Teagan opened the kitchen drawer to get the wine opener.

"Not much to tell besides the kids are in school, and Christian's working nonstop."

Sasha popped the lid off and poured a small amount in a crystal wine glass. They clinked both glasses, and Teagan took a sip before placing it down on the table.

"Same with Stuart. I barely see him anymore until dinner time," Sasha remarked.

"He's an ad executive, right?" Teagan said.

Sasha nodded, gulped down the wine, and poured more into her glass.

"Don't remind me. I think he's having an affair," Sasha whispered and drank the rest down.

"What makes you think that?"

"I just have a feeling. He's sneaky and never answers his phone when I'm around."

"Stuart loves you, Sasha."

Sasha waved off her admission.

"What would you do if your husband were keeping secrets from you?" Sasha questioned. Teagan shot her a confused look. None of her close friends or family knew what she did in the Navy, except for Christian. Teagan now sensed something was amiss with Sasha bringing up all these thoughts after so many years. Teagan leaned back in her chair, crossed her legs, and raised her arm on the back of the chair.

"I trust my husband. Has Stuart ever given you a reason not to?"

"You remember that time I told you about this guy I met at the store who hit on me?" Sasha said.

"Did you cheat on Stuart?" Teagan whispered.

"No, but I did give him my number." Sasha covered her face with both hands in embarrassment.

"Wow."

"You think I'm a slut, don't you?"

"I think I need more wine."

"Tell the truth, Teagan. You have this perfect marriage with Christian. Tell me your secrets to happiness."

Teagan shrugged her shoulders.

"Honestly, I don't have an answer for you."

Sasha tapped her fingers on the wine glass and stared back at Teagan.

"I got a phone call from Abe Price today," Sasha mentioned, and Teagan stiffened at her words.

"Who are you?" Teagan gritted her teeth.

Sasha smirked, finished her wine, and sat forward in her chair.

"I'm your best friend or your worst enemy. You choose." Sasha stood as Christian and Stuart walked into the kitchen, laughing together. Sasha jumped up and kissed Teagan on the cheek, wrapping her arms around her for a hug.

"I'll be in touch, bestie," Sasha said.

"Honey, are you ready to head out? SJ is getting tired," Stuart spoke.

"That boy of mine is always interrupting my fun. It was good seeing you two again," Sasha stated and hugged Christian.

"Yeah, we'll be in touch," Teagan responded and walked them out and watched as they got in the car to leave. Sasha winked back at her and waved goodbye. Christian wrapped his arms around her waist and waved goodbye.

Chapter Thirteen

The next day, Teagan was in Christian's office on the computer early in the morning, researching Sasha and Stuart. She'd known them for about six years, ever since they moved in the neighborhood, and their kids went to the same school as CJ and Cole. Not being able to sleep all last night, Teagan tossed and turned until she decided to get ahead of whatever Sasha was trying to accomplish. The good thing about being the director of The Firm was that she had access to certain databases of the government, not only getting license information, background checks, and even medical records if need be.

"Born in Chicago," Teagan muttered, writing down the last known address Sasha had before getting married to Stuart.

As she read through the files, her cell phone rang.

"Yeah."

"They haven't left home since I got here," Daughtrey responded.

"No visitors in or out?" Teagan asked.

"No. What's going on, Teagan?" Daughtrey questioned.

"Right now, it's nothing, but I need to know if someone comes to visit or they leave."

"This is your best friend, right, and her husband?" Daughtrey said.

Teagan bit her bottom lip and groaned in frustration.

"I know it might seem extreme, but I have a bad feeling."

"What's your gut telling you?"

"She's working for someone, and we need to find out before we kill her."

"Are you sure you're able to do that knowing she's your best friend?"

"It's her family or mine."

"I understand, but this would look bad. It would bring in a lot of questions about you and what we do."

"I know. That's why I want to keep her under surveillance for now."

"Okay, boss. Whatever you say." Daughtrey ended the call. Teagan placed the phone on the desk and rubbed her temples. She stared at the screen of the family photos from social media of Sasha and Stuart during Christmastime. All those years of laughing and talking with a close friend, thinking if she slipped and told something she shouldn't have. Everything was coming full circle at the worst time for her while the news broke of the agency.

"Hey, what are you doing up so early?" Christian strolled in his office, and Teagan hurriedly clicked the screen to a spades game on the computer.

"I couldn't sleep, so I decided to come in here and play some games."

Teagan rose, stretched her arms, and leaned up to peck him on the lips.

"Is this the case you're working?"

"Are the kids up?"

"Not yet. I was about to start breakfast," Christian responded, and Teagan pulled out of his arms and changed the subject.

"Let me start on breakfast, and you get the kids up and ready for school."

"Sounds good, but I need to head to the office right after. Can you get the kids to school for the day?" Christian asked, and Teagan nodded, tightening her robe around her waist and heading toward the kitchen. He grasped her arm and pulled her back to this chest.

"I love you," Christian said and pressed a kiss to her lips.

"I love you too," Teagan replied and smiled.

Getting the kids off to school was one of the best days that Teagan missed as a stay-at-home mom. Hearing about their teachers, friends, and new things they'd learned was a highlight she enjoyed as they piled out of the car to preschool. Once they got safely inside, she drove toward work to continue researching Sasha and Stuart in case she tried to contact her again. Getting into traffic, she turned the radio up, listening to the weather report. Her Bluetooth was connected when the phone rang.

"Hello."

"Agent Stone, this is Abe Price."

"Hello, Mr. Price, how can I help you?"

Teagan turned at the light and continued driving on Third Avenue and Lincoln.

"I just wanted to thank you again for the information."

"You're welcome, but I don't expect this to be an ongoing relationship, Mr. Price."

"I figured that, but did you see the updates about Congress wanting to investigate Fenton's death?"

"No, that's news to me."

"Can you confirm or deny any involvement in his death?" Abe asked.

Teagan chuckled and shook her head as she turned in the back of The Firm building. Security checked her car and allowed entry after scanning her fingerprint for verification.

"I cannot verify or deny anything about Ambassador Fenton."

"You're good."

Driving in the garage, Teagan parked in the reserved spot for employees.

"Mr. Price, I'm doing my job, and I suggest you do yours. The ambassador was a troubled man, and I wish his family nothing but peace."

"Is that on record?"

"You never stop, do you?"

"My job, Agent Stone."

"I understand that. Let me go off to do mine, and I hope you have a good day," Teagan responded and turned the car off. She grabbed her briefcase and badge to head up the elevator to her office. Five minutes later, she got off and noticed her office door open already. She slowly pushed it wider and saw Broderick sitting in her chair.

"What are you doing in my office?" Teagan placed her briefcase and purse down on the chair and pushed his feet off her desk.

"We need to talk." Broderick stood and walked around her desk to stand in front of her.

"About?"

"Are you planning to bring me up on charges?" Broderick asked.

"To be honest, you're the last thing on my mind, Broderick."

"What does that mean?"

"It means I have many enemies, and you're one of the last for me to deal with." Teagan strolled around and sat in her chair.

"Like whom?" he asked.

"Possibly the president. Plus, my longtime best friend may be a spy as well." Teagan motioned her hands in the air.

"Damn."

"Yeah, so forgive me if I'm not in the mood."

"Is there anything I can help with?"

"Not right now."

"What's her name?"

"Sasha."

Broderick nodded and turned to march out of her office, Teagan started all over again in reading about the early years of The Firm. Stanton was corrupt, but she didn't want to only bring light to his injustices if the entire political beast could be crumbled. Then she'd done her job correctly.

Chapter Fourteen

Teagan closed the car door, walked around to the driver's side, and climbed in. She checked the rearview mirror and noticed the same woman from inside the grocery store who seemed to be at every aisle they stopped on. Teagan shook it off that it was just a coincidence, nothing more, and started her car. Checking the back mirror, she put her car in reverse, heading to the stop sign that led onto the main street.

"Mommy, tell Cole I get to pick the movie today," Tatum said, with her arms folded and lip poked out. Early this morning when Teagan woke her up for the day, she wanted two large ponytails on both sides of her head with red bows tied on the ends. She was the only girl and spoiled rotten. Teagan and Christian promised themselves that after the two boys, they wouldn't want another child because of their busy careers. Traveling more with The Firm and taking on heavy cases that dealt with more violence, she'd promised herself to not put more stress on herself and focus more on being a mom and wife. Then after a surprise pregnancy while they were on vacation six years ago, a wide-eyed, brown-skinned, and button-nosed little baby came along, which changed their minds and proved to be the spark the family was missing all along.

Teagan continued driving, listening to the kids go back and forth about which one cleaned their room better. Teagan glanced over to the left side mirror and noticed a black minivan driving in and out of traffic. The same woman from the grocery store the other day was talking on the phone. Teagan peered up into the car's rearview mirror. Both kids weren't paying attention to what was happening around them as their mother changed lanes to see if the car was following them or not. Teagan sped up a little when Tatum screamed in the backseat.

"Mommy!" Tatum shouted.

"Cole, leave your sister alone," Teagan called out as the same black minivan changed lanes to continue following them. Teagan reached over to the passenger seat, pulled her phone out of her purse, and texted Spider.

"Mommy, can we have pizza tonight?" Cole asked.

"Yes, baby," Teagan replied, not paying attention to the conversation.

Teagan: Black minivan 678JHG

Spider: Where are you?

Teagan: Fifteen minutes from home

Spider: How many people?

Teagan: One woman, 5'8, blond hair, short bob

Spider: When did you first see her?

Teagan: Inside the store.

"I want tacos, Mommy," Tatum blurted out, lifting her doll up to show off to her brother. Teagan continued to peer over at the car behind them when a new notification came through from Spider.

Spider: I have Gregory running the plates.

Teagan: I'm turning off on my street now.

The car turned right abruptly as Teagan headed down the street and pulled into her driveway. Teagan turned the car off and glanced around her neighborhood. One car was parked two blocks down from her next-door neighbor. Teagan calmly removed the keys from the ignition, put on a big smile, and turned to the kids in the backseat.

"Are we ready to watch a movie?" Teagan asked.

"Yayyy!" They both screamed excitedly and clapped their hands. Teagan removed her seatbelt, grabbed her purse, and stepped out of the driver's side to help the kids out. Teagan kissed Tatum on her cheek and lifted the groceries out of the back trunk, letting Cole hold the house keys to open the front door. She peered over her shoulder at the black BMW parked. After Cole unlocked the door with Tatum's help, Teagan placed the bags down on the table and walked toward her bedroom closet. She bent down to remove the safe from the back corner. Typing in the password, she removed her gun and burner phone. She texted Spider once again to get an updated status.

Teagan: Home, Black BMW

Spider: Five minutes out.

Teagan: Park around the block, come through back.

Spider: Copy.

"Mommy, I'm hungry," Cole yelled from his bedroom.

Teagan checked to make sure she had a full clip in her gun, then placed it behind her back and covered under her shirt.

"Give Mommy a few minutes. I'll grab you a snack."

"Can we have pizza?" Tatum asked.

"No, we're having baked chicken and vegetables," Teagan replied.

Teagan heard both kids groan in disappointment, and she smiled. As she walked back in the living room and carried the groceries into the kitchen. Teagan grabbed yogurt out of the fridge for both kids and strolled back to Cole's bedroom.

"I need you both to stay here until I tell you to come out, okay?"

"What's wrong, Mommy?" Tatum asked, lifting her head to stare at Teagan as she opened the carton of yogurt. Teagan pressed a kiss on her forehead.

"Nothing, baby, but don't come out of this room, okay?"

"Okay," Tatum said.

"Good. Dinner will be ready soon," Teagan said, leaving the bedroom and shutting the door. With a sigh, Teagan thought over a quick plan of keeping her kids safe in case Spider didn't make it in time. Christian was with CJ at basketball practice, and she wasn't expecting them home until dinner. A knock on the door pulled her from her thoughts. Teagan turned on her heels and looked out the side window at the man standing in front of her door wearing all black. She checked her watch and went back to the kids' door to make sure they were preoccupied. Another knock on the door came with authority. Feeling like this wasn't the place to have a shootout, Teagan decided to stay calm and talk as long as she could to give Spider enough time to get to her home.

Knock! Knock!

Teagan opened the door.

"Yes, can I help you?" Teagan said, staring at the man who stood around six-foot-three, with a thin build and a crooked smile on his face.

"Teagan Stone?" he asked.

"Yes," Teagan replied.

"I need you to come with me," he spoke.

"Who are you?" Teagan gripped the doorknob.

"I work for the government. Jesus Morenz," he responded, lifting his badge.

"I'm sorry. You must have the wrong house," Teagan said, started to close the door. He wedged his foot to stop it.

"I don't think so," Jesus sated.

Teagan glared at him and moved her hand to her back, ready to lift her gun when Tatum interrupted, "Mommy!"

Tatum screamed as Spider knocked another man on the head with the butt of his gun as he tried to grab Tatum. Teagan turned, ready to shoot from the distress in her daughter's voice when

Jesus reached over and grabbed her from behind. Teagan stomped her foot down on Jesus to get loose and head butted him.

"Arghh!" Jesus yelled and let Teagan go to rub his forehead from the pain. Teagan punched him in the face and lifted her leg to kick him, but he grabbed her before making contact and slammed her down on the floor.

"Fuck!" she shouted.

"Mommy!" Cole ran out of the room, trying to help Tatum off the floor.

"Go to your room, Cole, and close the door." Teagan's breath came out in short spurts. Jesus wrapped his hands around her neck. Teagan reached up and gouged at his eyes. To get enough room between them, she bit his right wrist and bent it back as she went behind him and placed her arms around his neck. His breath hitched.

"Who sent you?" Teagan barked out.

Spider knocked the other man down on the ground. Teagan squeezed even harder to get Jesus to submit to her questions. The door opened, and Christian and CJ walked inside, laughing.

"Babe!" Christian called out, holding CJ's bags.

Teagan looked up abruptly, startled as CJ tried to look around his dad at what was going on.

"Christian, get him out of here," Teagan spoke. Spider called in for backup. Teagan watched as Christian pushed CJ outside towards the front door and ran down the hallway to get to his other kids. Spider held his gun at an unconscious Jesus as Teagan let him go.

"Who are they?" Spider questioned.

"I don't know," Teagan answered.

Christian hugged Tatum as he held her in his arms and she cried. Cole stood at his side.

"What the hell do you mean you don't know!" Christian shouted, placing Tatum down on the floor and telling her to stand next to her brothers outside. More backup came, and local police arrived as sirens went off.

"Christian, I don't know. We just came back from the store," Teagan said, checking his pants pockets for ID. Spider walked over to the door as the police and Gregory approached.

"You promised this wouldn't come to our front door," Christian argued. Teagan wanted to say she lied, but the life she led was always changing at any moment. Christian knew this when he decided to ask for her hand in marriage. Teagan's career had been the most important part of who she was before she had kids and became a wife.

"Christian, we can talk about this later," Teagan spoke and passed the wallet over to Spider.

"No, we're going to talk about this now," Christian responded and marched over to Teagan and Spider with his back to the front door as the police walked inside. The paramedics marched in and went to check on Jesus.

"We can talk about this later," Teagan said, taking a deep breath. Christian shook his head in frustration and stepped away to tend to the kids. Deciding it would be a good idea to take them to a hotel while the police wrapped up the events of this afternoon, Christian grabbed their hands and walked them over to his car.

"Christian Hawkins," the blond woman from the grocery store who followed Teagan yelled as he shut the back passenger door. Teagan stepped off the porch, noticing the woman approaching her husband.

"Do I know you?" Christian said and removed his car keys from his pocket.

"I wanted to introduce myself," she said.

"Who are you?" he asked.

"I'm Sandra Gregg, reporter for GHC News," Sandra mentioned, pulling out her business card.

"I don't understand," Christian said.

"Your wife is the director of The Firm, an underground government agency," Sandra said.

"Why were you following me in the store?" Teagan said.

"Mrs. Stone," Sandra said, reaching her hand out for a shake.

"Mrs. Hawkins," Teagan remarked, hands crossed over her chest.

"Yes, sorry about that earlier," Sandra said.

"I need to get the kids away from here," Christian told her.

They stared into each other's eyes.

"Okay." Teagan watched as he got in the car and drove off.

"I'd like to interview you," Sandra requested.

"No," Teagan responded and started to leave when Sandra grasped her arm.

Teagan glanced down at her arm.

"I can do the story with or without you," Sandra said, as the paramedics left the house. Sandra removed her hand.

"There's no story to tell."

"My viewers would say differently. You came back after being gone for a few years to lead a team across the globe to stop the election of the prime minister," Sandra explained.

"I'm not doing this with you." Teagan continued toward her house.

"Mrs. Stone, I can be a good ally for your team, or your worst enemy," Sandra warned, walking behind Teagan.

"Sandra, if you ever come to my house again, or follow my children without my permission, I will make sure I'm not the only one who ends up gone."

Sandra smirked, lifting a brow.

"Are you threatening me?" Sandra questioned.

"I don't make threats. I am the threat," Teagan said and shut the door in Sandra's face. Standing in her living room, she glanced around at the mess that was made. She knew a conversation would be had between her and Christian. The kids were never to be exposed to her life outside of being just their mom. The police taking the two men into custody would more than likely lead to more questions and answers she couldn't give. The only thing to do was to make sure they didn't make it to lockup. This was a part of the job she didn't like, but it needed to be done if she wanted to continue protecting The Firm.

"Make the call," Teagan ordered.

"Are you sure?" Gregory replied.

"Make the call," Teagan responded.

"She's going to be a problem," Spider said, pointing to the door. Teagan looked out of the peep hole as Sandra walked back to her car.

"Keep someone on her."

"A reporter, Teagan. The president won't like that," Spider announced.

"My job is to keep the country safe. The president came to me," Teagan said. She removed her gun, set it down on the table, and sent a message to her husband.

Teagan: I love you.

Christian: I know.

Teagan wanted to be with her family right now but seeing her kids once again in harm's way was too close for comfort, and unfortunately, she had to deal with the cleanup. As the director, she was in charge of making sure everything was documented and presented to the president. Now that a reporter had contacted her family, Teagan knew things could only get more complicated, but she had to focus on getting her home back in order and calling her husband and kids before they went to bed. The life of a spy never got easier when you added in being a wife and a mother.

"What are you thinking?" Spider questioned.

"I think this is only the beginning," Teagan replied, pushing the table back to its original position. Then she headed to the kitchen and saw the backdoor. She realized how Jesus' partner came in and went straight to Cole's bedroom.

"Only the beginning," Teagan repeated, standing at the bedroom door with her hands in her pockets, peering around the room in thought.

The End...

Check out a sneak peek at Agent Red-Fatal Crime Book #3 on my website!

Reading Order of Series

1.Agent Red-Fatal Memory Book 1
https://books2read.com/u/4j2PYX
2.Agent Red-Fatal Target Book 2
https://books2read.com/u/bWP8Jq
3.Agent Red-Fatal Crime Book 3
https://books2read.com/u/mZadZJ
4.Agent Red-Fatal Justice Book 4
https://books2read.com/u/mq07wd

Can she solve a fatal crime in time, or will it leave her open to more enemies?

Join the mailing list for sneak peeks and order at the link below.

www.authoravasking.com

What's Next?

Want to know what happens next? Follow me at the links below to catch the next release.

Thank you so much for reading, and if you enjoyed the crazy ride and decided to leave a review, we'd appreciate the support. Reviews are the lifeblood of the publishing world. They're read, appreciated, and needed. Please consider taking the time to leave a few words on Goodreads or BookBub.

Sign up for updates and sneak peeks at the sites below:

www.authoravasking.com
    www.bookbub.com/authors/ava-s-king
    www.goodreads.com/author/show/19855864.Ava_S_King
    www.twitter.com/authoravaking
    www.instagram.com/authoravasking
    www.facebook.com/authoravaking
    304publishing.tumblr.com

Acknowledgments

I want to thank my team, who helps me behind the scenes, from my editors to my test readers and graphic designers, and the list goes on. I appreciate each of you for keeping me on my toes.

About the Author

Ava S. King is the debut author of thriller, mystery, suspense, and psychological crime novels.

If you want to know when the next book will come out, please visit Author Ava S. King website at www.authoravasking.com, where you can sign up to receive an email for her next release.

About 304 Publishing Company

We showcase authors writing African American, interracial, women's fiction, urban romance, erotica, and contemporary romance novels, along with thrillers, suspense novels, poetry collections, and beauty & style books.

Join our mailing list to stay updated with new releases and blog posts.

www.authoravasking.com

www.ingramcontent.com/pod-product-compliance
Lightning Source LLC
Chambersburg PA
CBHW071837190726
48292CB00005B/1804